FOR EACH HEART BROKEN,
ANOTHER DREAM COMES TRUE . . .

JESS—His heritage made him Yussel Rabinovitch, cantor. But he wanted to sing for millions—to be Jess Robin, superstar.

CANTOR RABINOVITCH—Bitter with grief, Jess's father wondered: Did God save his family from war-time death so that Jess could turn his back on God?

RIVKA—Jess's wife. Proud to be the wife of a cantor. But afraid to be the wife of a rock star.

MOLLY—Jess's manager. The woman whose love changed his life.

THE JAZZ SINGER

THE JAZZ SINGER

RICHARD WOODLEY

Based on the Screenplay by
HERBERT BAKER

Adaptation by
STEPHEN H. FOREMAN

Based on the Play by
SAMSON RAPHAELSON

CORGI BOOKS
A DIVISION OF TRANSWORLD PUBLISHERS LTD

THE JAZZ SINGER
A CORGI BOOK 0 552 11741 2

First publication in Great Britain

PRINTING HISTORY
Corgi edition published 1981

ACKNOWLEDGMENTS
Grateful acknowledgment is made for permission to
reprint the following copyright material:

  Lines from "America" by Neil Diamond; copyright ©
1980 by Stonebridge Music. All rights reserved.
  Lines from "Hello Again", words by Neil Diamond and
music by Neil Diamond and Alan Lindgren; copyright ©
1980 by Stonebridge Music. All rights reserved.
  Lines from "Love on the Rocks" by Neil Diamond and
Gilbert Becaud; copyright © 1980 by Stonebridge Music
and EMA-Suisse. All rights reserved.
  Lines from "Songs of Life" by Neil Diamond and
Gilbert Becaud; copyright © 1980 by Stonebridge Music
and EMA- Suisse. All rights reserved.
  Lines from "You Baby" by Neil Diamond; copyright
© 1980 by Stonebridge Music. All rights reserved.
  Lines from "Little Green Apples" by Bobby Russell;
copyright © 1968 by Bibo Music Publishers, c/o the
Welk Music Group, Santa Monica, Ca. 90401.
International copyright secured. All rights reserved.
Used by permission.
  Line from "You Are My Sunshine" by Jimmie Davis
and Charles Mitchell: copyright 1940 by Peer International
Corporation, renewed by Peer International Corporation.
All rights reserved. Used by permission of Peer
International Corporation and Southern Music Inc.
  Line from "The St. Louis Blues," published by Handy
Brothers Music Company; copyright 1914 W. C.
Handy, renewed © 1942 by W. C. Handy. All rights
reserved, including the right of public performance for
profit. By permission of the publisher.

Corgi Books are published by Transworld Publishers Ltd.
Century House, 61–63 Uxbridge Road, Ealing,
London W5 5SA

Made and printed in the United States of America

THE JAZZ
SINGER

Chapter 1

Jess was too nervous to worry about how the service had gone. If his high notes cracked occasionally, well, it never hurt to have a little cry in your voice. So few people to hear it anyway. His prayer shawl had brown stains on it. There was a leak in the pipes above the dresser, and the silk had become damp and spotted. He tossed the shawl over a hanger to air it and let it dry completely.

There were voices in the hallway. He had no time to chat. He couldn't be late, even though he'd rather not show up at all. The whole prospect made him nervous. Plus he shouldn't have been so preoccupied throughout the prayer service, thinking about this stupid gig. But it was important. He could have laughed at what a fraud he was, or was about to become, except that he was too nervous and likely to be late.

The voices came closer. Jess snatched up his guitar case and hurried out the side door.

There wasn't any good way to get to the West Side except to run. He wasn't about to cough up three bucks for a cab. Lucky it wasn't raining, lucky it wasn't so warm, on this May evening, as to boil up an immediate sweat. He jogged as smoothly as possible without jarring his guitar.

Hard to jog and think at the same time, which was good because Jess didn't want to think about it; bad because he collided with a pushcart coming around the corner, its proprietor head-down against what might have been a wind but was probably the weight of a long day.

Jess bounced lightly off the silver hot-dog cart, slick as a dancer, spun to the side, continued across the intersection.

"Schmuck!" he heard a couple of seconds later when the vendor was apparently certain that Jess wasn't going to stop for a confrontation.

He dropped down the steps at the entrance to the IND line, slid a token into the turnstile, and sprang through the closing doors of the local. He stood his guitar case between his legs and sagged back against the doors for the short ride uptown.

He brushed his soft brown hair back over his ears with his fingers and let a sigh whistle through his closed teeth. What a crazy idea. Money, fortune, fame —what a crock. Friendship was all he was doing it for. That and fifty cents would get him a ride back home. He almost got out at the first stop. But Bubba would be waiting for him, and he couldn't just flat stand him up. He would at least show up and tell him it was too crazy an idea. Guilt Jess could handle; he wasn't into humiliation. Bubba would understand. Friendship didn't need this.

He got out at West Fourth Street and stomped up the stairs toward the lights of Greenwich Village. If Bubba wasn't there, right there at the entrance waiting for him, Jess wouldn't spend one minute looking, he'd turn right around and go home.

Bubba was there, leaning casually against the newsstand, unlit cigarette dangling between his lips, his neatly picked Afro reflecting its sheen under the street-lamp, his strong arms folded across his chest.

Bubba nodded slowly, Jess shook his head just as slowly. They slapped palms and Bubba took Jess's free arm and steered him across the avenue.

"You look like you hurried," Bubba said, chuckling.

"It's never gonna work."

"It's gonna work. You better take that pancake off your head."

Jess touched the top of his head and discovered that he had forgotten to remove his yarmulke after the service. He quickly tucked the skullcap into his pocket. "It's never gonna work."

"It's gonna work."

Jess was used to the incredible mix of styles and people that characterized the Greenwich Village section of New York: bums and Bohemians, artists, students, aunts and uncles and children, beards and sandals, suits and ties, every imaginable ethnic representation, age, coloration, disposition, in the area that included every imaginable destination from fine, quaint row houses on narrow, cozy streets to the most raucous clubs and haunts and head shops. He had known it since he was a child; he and Rivka had courted around here; Jess had hung out by himself or with friends to listen to music. The Village was, as such outlandish areas and sights and circumstances become to established New Yorkers, commonplace.

But tonight Jess suddenly saw it differently. At that moment it was all masks and disguises and hidden missions. For a moment he found himself wondering just who everybody was and where everybody was going. And suddenly it was himself he was wondering about, another mask and disguise, a crazy incognito mission when he should be home chatting to Rivka about how their day had been.

Abruptly he stopped. "It's no good, Bubba. If it's gonna work, it's gonna work without me. I'm out." He turned back toward the subway.

Bubba put a heavy hand on his shoulder and gave him a crooked grin. "With you, my man. Why it's gonna work is because it's fifty bucks. Five tens for what you usually do for free, for what we did so long for kicks. So come on. Right around the corner here."

Bubba tugged his shoulder, and Jess hunched against the strong hand and grunted as he followed. They stopped in front of a red-painted stone building the street floor of which had broad, dingy, curtained windows. The plastic sign over the windows was lit up with flickering letters that said CINDERELLA CLUB.

"So," Bubba said, gesturing grandly. "All we gotta do is do it. Listen, my man." He took both Jess's shoulders and looked into his eyes. "Will you please trust me?"

"No."

"Good." Bubba grinned and pulled him toward the door. "Come on in!"

It was a small club, surprisingly busy and loud. They pushed quickly through the tables, sidling past the waiters carrying their trays high. The small stage at the rear, framed with cheap heavy blue curtains, was set up for musicians—drums, mikes, amplifiers, electric piano—but was otherwise empty.

"On a break," Bubba explained over his shoulder as he led the way through a curtained passage beside the stage and up the steps to the backstage area.

"I didn't figure it was an invisible band," Jess muttered.

A couple of house musicians, one white, one black, both dressed in gray, slouched on stools with smoke curling up from cigarettes that dangled in their fingers. They nodded at Bubba. A technician with long hair over his shoulders and a holster of tools on his hip worked around a circuitbreaker box. Back here, the noise of the crowd was muffled, but the odor of liquor and smoke was heavy. A hint of pine scent suggested the proximity of deodorized restrooms.

"Where's Molly?" Bubba asked one of the musicians.

The musician nodded toward the wings, where a woman was emerging, glancing back over her shoulder in the direction of the crowd and then shaking her head. Her long dark curly hair fluffed gently, at odds with the severity of her black pantsuit. Her step was lively, her smile pretty, and she wrinkled her nose.

"Why is it I feel like I'm in a wild West saloon in here?" she asked no one in particular. "Rough bunch of dudes out there. Waiters oughta be drawing combat pay. Not gonna be easy to blow out this crowd. Bubba!"

"Hey, sweetness."

"It's a great audience, Bubba, they're gonna love you!"

They hugged warmly, then Molly pulled back and leaned over to look past Bubba at Jess. "Is this him?"

"My man, Jess Robin."

Molly extended her arm, sighted over her raised thumb like an artist examining perspective. "Perfect. Not too big, not too small. He'll fit right in."

"Jess," Bubba turned to him, holding Molly's arm, "this is Molly Oliver, our manager. Lady can really get down. Lady of ideas, Jess, and this was one of her best."

"Your idea," Jess said, cocking his head.

"Yup."

"You're crazy."

Her look became more serious. "Why? Bubba tells me you wrote their opening, you know all their charts, plus Bubba tells me you got a baritone can make green fruit ripe."

"Exactly what I told her, Jess, the truth."

"This ain't no orchard here."

"No, but it's dark." Bubba put an arm around his shoulders and spoke confidentially. "Dark enough, my man. We'll try and keep the spots off you, you just stay in the shadows much as you can. Lot of smoke out there. Everybody a little boozed, a little high, just wanting to ride on some of those good sounds we do—dig?"

"People also gonna have their eyes closed?"

"People see what they wanna see." He looked up toward the dressing room. "Hey, dig the rest of the family."

Bubba's brothers, Mel and Timmy, sauntered out. They wore dark green suits and bright orange lapels and mint-green shirts open at the collar, and black patent leather boots with platform soles. They resembled Bubba, with broad faces and broad shoulders, but were not as large. Mel carried a sax, Timmy a bass guitar.

Seeing Jess, Mel stopped short, then came quickly over, beaming, to skin palms. "Hi, brother! Looking fine!"

"Mel, Timmy." Jess slapped palms with both of them unenthusiastically.

They headed off to the wings, Jess watching them. He shook his head slowly.

"Lighten up, my man."

"That's not exactly my problem, Bubba."

"Well, I mean—"

"No, no, no. It's weird, this whole business. Just too weird. You know?"

"Sure it's weird." Bubba spread his arms. "Life is weird. Right? So, I mean, this is just one of the weird parts of the weird. We finally get to audition for all these dudes and Teddy has to go and get busted. That's not weird? I mean, he gets busted right *now,* when we get our break. Six months, he gets, may have to serve one of them. Why one of my own brothers gotta get busted right now? This is prime time, he gets sent away for. And for what? For parking a car in his own garage."

"For parking somebody else's car, to be precise, Bubba."

"Yeah, well, you talk about weird, that's weird. Could of been a year ago, or a year from now, that's cool. But now. Then we would've been together for this gig, and be off and running. Well, what goes around comes around, and where you got bad luck you also got good. The good is you been part of our scene, and you're more than good enough. With a little protective coloration, as they say in the jungle business."

Jess sighed.

Molly took his elbow. "Come here." She tugged him off to the wings, nudged the curtain aside, and pointed to one of the front tables. "See that little guy there?" She spoke in a stage whisper.

"They all look little, sitting down."

"Right there, third table from the left, the little paunchy guy."

"With the mustache."

"That's him. He's Eddie Gibbs. He's big."

"He's little."

"I mean," she gave him a playful slap on the arm, "he's an agent from the Morris office, their Los Angeles office. He just got in from the Coast and I was lucky enough to get him down here. Now the point is, I got him to come here to catch a hot new act with four brothers. 'Hot new act' means nothing to him. Neither does 'brothers.' But 'four brothers,' he bit on that. So we've got to give him four brothers. See?"

"You, that's what I see." He smiled thinly. "You look too nice to be in this business."

"Don't kid yourself, buster. So do you, by the way. But they'll fix that in the dressing room." She turned and signaled. "He's yours, Bubba."

"Look, Bubba," Jess said, again finding himself propelled under Bubba's strong arm, "now you got the guy here, why don't you tell him the truth? And for the rest of the bozos out there, you can just fake the number with three."

Bubba chuckled as he shoved Jess through the dressing-room door. "We're already faking it with four. And I mean faking it, my man! But one thing you learn on the street: you're gonna fake something, don't fake the numbers. Four is the truth, *brother!*"

Molly stepped between Mel and Timmy, who were fiddling with their instruments. "Listen, guys, play everything to Gibbs, he's the only one we care about. And no matter what happens, keep smiling."

"Smiling we do good." Timmy chortled.

"What can happen?" Mel asked.

Molly cocked her head. "Well, it's the Cinderella Club. From the looks of it, they don't turn into pumpkins, they throw 'em."

"We'll smile," Timmy said, strumming a few notes.

Molly leaned back against the wall and folded her arms and stared at the dressing-room door. Nice-looking guy, she was thinking, nice brown eyes, nice cleft chin, nice smile, nice hands. On the small side, but lean, athletic. Sexy too, how he walked. But more important than any of that was if he could sing. She hoped like hell he could sing. Or if not, that he could just mouth the words and keep good time on his rhythm guitar. She'd had some successes in the past, pulled off some lucky gigs. But she'd never tried something so outlandish as this. People said she had un-squelchable optimism. She didn't. She just knew there was no point in being pessimistic. Enough went wrong without looking for it. She was realistic. And that meant you kept plugging. Whether or not you *were* optimistic, in this business if you didn't *seem* like you were, you were dead. So far she was alive. This was one of those nights when you counted the minutes.

She went over and peeked through the curtains. Damn place was jammed. And not too friendly. The show was starting late. She heard the rustling behind her as the musicians took their places on the dark stage. The audience sounded like a union hall taking a strike vote. Loud voices, stamping feet. She wondered whether the large number of black faces among the crowd portended good or ill. She closed her eyes and heard the announcer's mike rasp and clack as he tapped his finger on it. Then the drum roll quieted the mob and the announcer leaned into it:

"It's sho-o-ow time!" There were some boos and catcalls, a few cheers, one singularly articulated "Whoopee!"

"Ladies and gentlemen! The Cinderella Club, right here in the heart of New York's Greenwich Village, famed for..." More catcalls drowned out the rest of the phrase, then quieted. "... the Cinderella Club is proud to present a great new group, their first time on a New York stage—ladies and gentlemen, for your pleasure, the *Brothers Four!*"

Molly opened her eyes to slits just as the first spotlight came on to hit the far end of the group, fixing Timmy in his set pose, smiling broadly. Then the second spot came on, fixing Mel posed the same—hip cocked, one foot forward, also smiling. Then the third light hit Bubba, standing a half step in front of the others. Finally the fourth light—Molly winced—shot out to fix Jess Robin, nearest her.

Jess's pose was slightly different, slightly less cocky, slightly less of a smile. But how different he really was Molly hoped only she could see. His face and hands were stained dark with vegetable dye, and he averted his face slightly from the crowd. Molly could tell, but she was closer than the first row. She glanced down at the nearest tables. Eddie Gibbs was sitting placidly. Jess looked black enough.

It had worked so far. Still, it was an eternity, that moment between the first smiles into the lights and Bubba's downbeat that snapped the group to action.

They swung smartly into a song Jess had written —"You, Baby"—a jazz-rocker impelled by a heavy up-tempo beat, Bubba's tenor taking the lead.

Jess filled nicely with his baritone, cautiously at first, managing to edge partly out of the light. Bubba carried the first verse, then stepped back with the others for the chorus: "...Move me, baby, like you're gonna save me..."

As always, the music seized Jess, took him over. Now his husky voice asserted itself more and more; his left fingers danced over the frets along the throat of his guitar while his right hand chopped down across the strings like an ebony hammer.

Heads in the audience began to bob in time, hands slapped tabletops. Molly clapped the rhythm in the wings.

During a brief instrumental passage, Bubba leaned to Jess. "You doing fine, my man."

Yes, he was. Jess felt the music well up in him, surge through him, a palpable force that was his creation, his to control. It was his music, his. He was flying.

Bubba took a step forward for his second solo lead. But Jess didn't let it go. He kept on, raising his voice, sliding effortlessly into the lead voice, taking over, singing Bubba's part.

"Hey, man," Bubba hissed out of the corner of his mouth, still smiling, "that's mine!"

Jess heard only his own voice, his music. He pounded on with the solo: "...Every little mood that moves me is you, babe; every little move is me for you..."

Bubba could do nothing but drop his own voice and step back with the others to fill behind the lead of Jess, continuing to smile and sway with the ensemble.

Molly sensed the trouble. Bubba was the lead. That Jess sang with beautiful force was not the point; she was a woman with a major strength in setting things up and seeing that they ran right. Something here was running wrong no matter how good it was. Wrong was trouble, in a place like this.

She scanned the audience; they were eating it up. Eddie Gibbs was leaning forward in his chair, tapping both knees with his hands.

Jess was beating out the final lines now, sweat gleaming on his forehead and chin. Bubba, long since resigned to letting Jess run with it, was now as pleased as the others at the big sound of the baritone lead, and was beating the tempo in the air with his fist.

A large black man under the spell of the music was moved to get up from his table and begin boogie-ing in the aisle. Muscles bulging under a silky shirt as he snapped his fingers and shimmied his shoulders, he boogied right up to the foot of the stage, eyes on Jess.

Jess played to the man, poured it on, and hit his final chord, whereupon a few beads of perspiration formed under his eyes and rolled down his cheeks, taking strips of black dye with them and leaving white streaks from eyes to lip.

The entire audience rose in applause and cheers for Jess and the music. Jess bowed, included the rest of the group in his gesture, then straightened up to find himself being stared at quizzically by the large black man standing in front of the stage.

The man's eyes widened in recognition as Jess's eyes narrowed warily.

"Uh-oh," Bubba muttered, watching.

As the cheering and applause died down, the man, fully six and a half feet tall, drew back his shoulders to exaggerate his barrel chest, clenched his hands, and bellowed: "Jive phony! Who you think you jivin'? You ain't no brother. Get that honkie off!"

Jess tried to step out of the lights toward the wings. The man leaned on the stage floor with his knuckles.

"That ain't off enough, honkie!" The man jumped

up onto the stage with the ease of one hopping over a curb.

"Now just cool it, mister," Jess said, holding up a palm and backpedaling while he slipped his guitar strap off over his head. "Okay?"

"Yeah, bro," Bubba said, heading over to intercept the black man, "just be cool, no harm no foul."

"I ain't paid no cover charge for no cover-up!" the man barked, snapping around toward Bubba and at the same time delivering a long, backhanded swipe that smacked across Bubba's cheek.

At almost the same instant, Jess was on the big man. First he hooked a left into the man's shoulder, turning him face-on. He threw a right into the cushy area just under the man's rib cage, hooked another left to the man's jaw, then followed with a straight right that sent him reeling back a couple of drunken steps before he sagged to his knees.

The first table to erupt was the one from which the black man had come, his three drinking buddies leaping for the stage. The three brothers and Jess met them head on. The thud and crack of solidly landing punches was lost amid the screaming and hollering from all over the room. Others, black and white, sprang to their feet, knocking over tables. Some of the wild audience headed for the stage, some squared off on the floor, some scrambled for the exits; waiters' trays spun loose, delivering their wares through the air like hailstones of glass.

The melee captured nearly everybody. While bodies tumbled and glasses shattered and sandwiches splatted throughout the club, Jess was leading the beset singing group on the stage—leading now with his fists. Light and quick on his feet, he swung punch after punch, each one landing with the damaging precision of the experienced street fighter. He dispatched one man coming straight at him, then spun to topple another heading for Bubba. Bubba had his hands full, literally, with headlocks clamped over two squirming victims. Another man dove at Jess's waist, but landed instead on Jess's sharply drawn-up knee.

One of the club musicians crouched behind the

electric piano started to hammer out "The Star-Spangled Banner" at full volume.

"Forget it!" Molly yelled, on her hands and knees beside him. "It only works for ball games!"

Then the piano was toppled over backward just as Molly scurried away to take refuge by ducking under the backdrop curtains.

Timmy managed to smash his guitar over the head of somebody coming at Jess with a broken bottle. Jess dropped a man in mid-leap with a right to the Adam's apple.

Molly peered out from under the back curtain, her eyes like twin moons on the horizon. "Give it to 'em!" she found herself hollering, swinging her hidden fists against the curtains. "Go, Jess!"

It was only a matter of minutes, but no sooner had the futile strains of the national anthem wailed to an inconclusive end than another wailing filled the room —police sirens.

Tires screeched outside. Uniformed cops swarmed through the front door, using their billy clubs with the customary skill of the N.Y.P.D., not swinging them wildly but holding them up with both hands to slap them under the chins of combatants, separate them, back them up.

The cops moved quickly through the room, pinning fighters this way and that, against the walls, back to back against each other, bent over upset tables. A team clambered up onto the stage, swatting at the backs of legs with their sticks, spearing deftly into chests, pushing and pinning, neatly dividing the warring factions.

"All right!" ordered a sergeant with professionally cool fervor. "Break it up! Everybody up against the wall! Move it!"

His men maneuvered their objects to the perimeter of the stage. Handcuffs ratcheted into place. Moans and groans and gasps were all that was left of the screaming and epithets and smashing of dishes. The policemen were beefy and strong; the only larger man on the stage was the black man who had started it all, and he, spread-eagled facing a wall, his palms up against it and his feet spread out behind him, was still sputtering with rage as the officer patted him down in a quick search.

"Man was *passing,* officer! Ain't got no right! Tough enough as it is out there without no new members of the damn race taking our spots! Honkie is a *fake!"*

"Clam up," said the officer, "and stand still."

"All right," said the sergeant, walking among them, "read these guys their rights. Everybody on the stage we're taking in."

There was a renewed surge of groans from the captives, the loudest from the three brothers.

"You heard him," one of the cops said wearily, pulling a wrinkled card out of his pocket, "so listen up. You all have the right to remain silent . . ."

Molly finally crawled from under the curtain and got to her feet. "Hey, officer!" She came trotting over to the sergeant, who regarded her with the interest of one seeing an approaching panhandler. "These guys, the brothers—the singers, I mean, the musicians—they were just acting in self-defense!" She touched his sleeve, then quickly withdrew her hand as he dropped his eyes to it. "See, they were just performing—they're big stars, *artists*—not one of them has ever been in any kind of trouble before, and they were just defending themselves. They almost got *killed!* So wouldn't it be in the best interest of justice if you just let them—"

"You!" It was Eddie Gibbs, in the firm grip of a lawman, big-time talent agent Eddie Gibbs, his shirt torn, a droplet of blood clinging to his nose, his whole body quivering and straining as if to get at her. "You . . . you . . ." His voice sputtered into a pathetic growl.

"Hi, Eddie! They were great, weren't they?" She gave him a cheerful smile, but her teeth chattered.

Eddie Gibbs howled like a hyena as the officer dragged him away.

"Well, the hell with him." She turned to Bubba, who was being hugged by the blue arm of a cop as if they were posing for an unhappy snapshot. "Listen, once we get Teddy back with the group, we'll go out to the Coast anyway. L.A.'s *my* home town."

"Out of the way, lady," the cop said as he started moving Bubba forward, " 'less you wanna join the party."

She fell in behind them, in front of Jess, whose captor cop was examining the white-streaked black face as if it were an ugly rash.

"Listen," she went on, "I've got some great ideas, Bubba . . ."

"For your sake," Jess called dryly to Bubba, "I hope she's got a better idea than tonight."

She dropped back beside Jess as the whole huffing and puffing parade moved toward the rear entrance. "Listen, Jess, it was unfortunate that this involved you, but these guys, the brothers, they're gonna get it together and make it, so I'd appreciate it if you—"

"You owe me fifty bucks."

"Forget it. That's your bail."

"Terrific."

"Listen, buster, not every manager would spring for that. You didn't finish the gig."

"I thought we cleaned it up pretty good."

"You know how to handle yourself, all right. Liked your singing, too."

"Well, you've seen my whole act. One show only. That's it. So do me a favor, Milly—"

"Molly."

"The next time you get a brainstorm—"

"Don't call us, we won't call you."

"You got it."

"Oh, I got it, all right," she said snippily, tilting her chin up, "and I'm not finished with it either. You'll see. These guys'll be gold."

Timmy raised his handcuffed fists buoyantly as the exit door was opened for him. "California, here we come!"

"Afraid it's not a direct flight," Jess muttered. "You got a layover in the cage."

"So what?" Bubba grinned as he turned his head back. "At least maybe we'll get a chance to lamp ol' Teddy in there. The family that plays together—"

"Stays together!" Mel chirped in.

"Say it, bro! Hey, officer, take it easy," Bubba said as they wedged through the door.

"You claiming police brutality?"

"You walking on my feet, that's all. Otherwise we all just cool and cooperative."

"Keep moving."

They were walked through the alleyway to the front and directed into the backseats of several police cars that were the center of attention of a rainbow of Village onlookers.

Jess was wedged in between a couple of cops.

" 'Smatter with your face?" one of them asked.

"Vegetable dye," Jess said matter-of-factly. "See? Health nuts ain't no healthier than anybody else."

Molly trotted along beside the cars as they started up. "Don't worry!" she called, giving them the thumbs-up. "I'll have you all out in the morning!"

"Who's the broad?" the cop asked.

"Fight promoter," Jess said.

"You being wise?"

"Not wise enough, I'm afraid."

"You look young. How old are you, early twenties?"

"Twenty-five."

"Just a kid. When I was your age—wouldn't hurt you to check in with a priest or minister or something, help put you on the track."

"First thing tomorrow, that's what I do."

"Good, good." The cop nodded with satisfaction. "If we can turn one young guy around, you know. And then a haircut, that wouldn't hurt."

"Right."

Jess picked up his wallet, keys, and a few dollars in cash, signed the form for the desk officer, and hurried out.

On the sidewalk, he took a deep breath of smoggy, hazy morning air.

So that was jail. Not so bad. Noise all night long—chatter, laughter, doors clanging, a minor dust-

up someplace with a recalcitrant prisoner. He hadn't
been able to sleep on the hard cot. Molly had bailed
them out, evidently, and he heard somebody say something about charges not being pressed. Once he had
washed his face in the cell, getting off most of the dye,
he had felt a little more normal, less of a curiosity in
everybody's eyes.

He chuckled, recalling Bubba saying to a guard,
"No matter how I wash and wash, it don't come
off."

Bubba was a stand-up guy, somebody you could
depend on, somebody you couldn't knock the spirit out
of. All these years, he had been the same, always
plugging away at his music—their music—never letting
the fates get him down, always figuring they'd make it
someday. Good bunch of friends, those brothers. No
sign of Teddy anyplace, but he was a survivor too.

Molly he couldn't figure. Pretty as she was, she
had a certain gritty air of toughness and confidence
about her. Attractive traits in general, but what the
hell was she doing with that gig last night?

His hands were a little stiff, bruised. But nobody
had touched his face. He had no swollen lips or sore
teeth or stiff jaw to bother his singing. So he would
sing this morning.

And it was with a degree of satisfaction that he
reviewed his extraordinary performance last night. He
had taken fencing lessons once, and that, combined
with his quick hands, good balance, and general fitness
—as well as his experience—served him well as always
when push came to shove. The music had been good
too.

He hailed a cab and directed it to an address on
the Lower East Side.

Jess did not often ride in a cab—or a car of any
kind, for that matter. City born and bred, he didn't
even know how to drive. It was odd, on this morning,
to be taking a cab, of all things, from jail, of all places,
to his own neighborhood. It was odd to see the familiar
streets in this way, from the back seat with the meter
ticking in front.

How much it had changed, the Lower East Side.

Young as he was, he still remembered when the several blocks around him were almost totally Jewish, when the streets were filled with pushcarts, when, at night, men, many or most of them in long black coats with black hats and pointed beards, would wander around or gather on the sidewalk in front of the delicatessens and candy stores and newsstands, speaking in Yiddish and waiting for an edition of the *Jewish Daily Forward*.

Whether the neighborhood was crumbling—as the newspapers said and as seemed true enough, given the rundown state of the buildings and how many were boarded up—or deteriorating, as residents said, meaning becoming a slum, the change was clear enough.

The Jews said they were being pushed out by the Chinese expanding from Chinatown to the west or the Puerto Ricans encroaching from the north. And then the blacks, of course, creeping in everywhere. Pushed or not, the young people were leaving. Jess had few friends left there. He and Rivka would move to a better neighborhood if they could. Well, maybe.

His father, of course, wanted them to stay. And Jess was not the type to desert. Like many of the young people, he was caught between ethnic ties and wanting better circumstances.

On this Thursday morning, these thoughts were neither here nor there; not relevant, because he was here and he was late.

They pulled up in front of a small synagogue, housed in a brownstone building whose building blocks were eroding, whose concrete steps were broken, whose single tree in front was barely clinging to life.

He paid the cabby and headed for the side entrance, glancing at the posted announcement of the morning's services that featured the name of Kalmen Rabinovitch, cantor.

He could hear his father's strong, rich tenor singing the blessings in the fine, vital style that mixed Hebrew words with Moorish inflections of music.

He stopped outside the door for a moment to listen. He rubbed his chin and realized he hadn't shaved. His fingers showed a bit of the dark stain from an unwashed spot. He took a deep breath and went in.

He went to the side room and hastily donned his cantorial robes, yarmulke, and now dry tallith, smoothing the fringe down straight. Then he tiptoed through the door of the anteroom and onto the dais.

Cantor Kalmen Rabinovitch, tall and proudly erect, glared briefly at his son through thick glasses without missing a note. Jess moved next to him and picked up the song, harmonizing with his baritone.

There was some nudging and nodding among the small congregation—mostly elderly men on the hard wooden benches—as they noted Jess's late entrance and rather unkempt appearance.

One stern face in the front row was that of Bernard Nussbaum, the lawyer and president of the men's group, a judgmental man itching with intolerance of what he assumed to be the lack of commitment on the part of the young assistant cantor, Jess. Next to him, more sorrowful than stern, was Jess's uncle Leo, his father's brother, who closed his eyes and gave a little shudder. Rabbi Birnbaum, at the other side of the dais, seemed not to notice, his eyes averted, his shoulders drooping under his robes.

As they sang, the cantor seemed to edge a step away from Jess. Jess could sense the anger, knew that it would pass, but knew as well that the deeper distress of his father for his son's life would remain.

The cantor picked up the Torah scroll to return it to the closetlike ark, and as he reached for it, Jess glimpsed the grim concentration camp tattoo on the underside of his father's wrist, bluish black like old veins that had given up their use and become gnarled into numbers.

The services ended. Jess turned immediately to his father, but the cantor stalked away from the pulpit and went into the anteroom, banging the door behind him.

Jess had paused and started to follow somberly when he saw Leo coming over, his familiar lumbering gait suggesting the carrying of a great weight.

"So," Leo said with mournful clarity, "how was jail?"

Jess blinked.

Leo raised his thick eyebrows as if repeating the question.

"Who told you?"

"Who told me." Leo shrugged. His tallith was yellowed with age. "Who told me? *He* told me." He waved toward the anteroom.

"My father? Who told him?"

"Not because she wanted to."

"Who?"

"A wife has to tell her father-in-law." It was like an indictment.

Jess stared at his uncle.

"Your own wife. Your own Rivka told him."

Jess dropped his eyes. Leo touched his arm and spoke more quickly, with a bit more warmth.

"Look, she'll explain everything to you, it's her way. She's been very worried. Naturally. Go . . ." he steered Jess toward the stairway, "she's still downstairs teaching class. Go to your Rivka."

They both pulled off their tallithim. Jess nodded and started away, but not without catching a glimpse of those awful little numbers etched in Leo's wrist too.

Chapter 2

Jess paused outside the classroom door and gazed through the clean glass pane.

Rivka was delivering an animated talk to the group of raptly attentive ten-year-olds.

Rivka had such energy, such intensity. Her curly black hair surrounded a fine-featured face. Her aquiline nose gave her a regal look, her wide mouth added sensuality. She was so dedicated, Rivka, so intelligent. He felt a pang of distance from her, her interests, her world. He was as dedicated as she, perhaps, but not in the same direction; he was not so intelligent or well read. Or at least not so knowledgeable. And she was so good with children. He too liked children, but he didn't have the touch. She doted on them. He was glad she had this outlet for her affections.

He rapped on the glass. She snapped her head around to see him, excused herself to the class, and hurried out.

"Yussel, Yussel," she said softly, immediately touching his face as if to make sure he was real. "Are you all right? Are you?"

Jess nodded and took her hand.

"Oh, Yuss, I've been so worried."

"I know. I'm sorry."

"Your hand." She looked down at his puffy right knuckles and then up into his eyes.

"Bruised, is all, I banged it up a little. Nothing else. I'm fine."

"So worried, what you get into . . ."

"I know. Uncle Leo told me. It was nothing serious, just a little hassle."

"What you call a little hassle . . ."

"How did Papa find out? I guess you told him."

She hunched her shoulders and held up her hands. "You called in the middle of the night. The same phone that woke me woke him. That's strange?"

"I didn't want you to worry, that's why I called."

"You call from jail, you don't want me to worry?"

"I told you I'd be all right."

"Oh, Yussel, what you call all right—"

"And I am all right."

"That's what I told him. I said Yussel's all right. I said you were spending the night with Bubba."

"I was. That's the truth." He smiled a little at the irony.

"So he knows you don't spend nights with Bubba —not that he would like it all that much if you did, you know how he feels. But I told him that."

"So?"

"So he didn't buy it. You think your father doesn't feel? No, he said, my son's wife doesn't come with a story. He wouldn't let me go back to sleep. He kept asking, what is it? 'A son calls in the middle of the night to tell his wife he's staying out.' He kept at me until I cracked. I'm no good at lying, Yussel."

"I'm sorry you had to. Was he angry at you?"

"Angry at me, your father? No, no, sad, I think, because I was upset. I couldn't hide it." She looked away, then back at him, her eyes drooping. "Oh, Yuss, I feel awful I wasn't there this morning."

"I wouldn't have wanted you to—"

"But you said that woman was bailing you out, and I had to leave for an early class—you know how Professor Hoffman is when you come late. And I need it for my thesis. It's so important. And I thought, 'Rivka, you have to get on with your work.' I couldn't help you there anyway, I guess."

"No, you did right."

"Then I had to be back here to teach Hebrew school, they count on me, and I'm always here on time—"

"Okay, okay."

She studied his face. "So how did Papa take it?"

"Lighthearted as always."

"You're being funny?"

"I'm sorry. I guess Papa's pretty upset. I guess he probably didn't like any of it. He would hardly look at me."

"I'm glad," she said firmly.

"Oh?" He cocked his head.

"I mean, that it came out in the open."

"Jail?"

"Not jail. You think I'm glad to know about jail? But the rest. I never liked your sneaking around like that, singing in those places."

"This was a little different. Besides," an edge crept into his voice, "you don't mind me making a little extra money."

"Extra money! I don't care how it comes? From what? Like maybe you should sell drugs to make some extra money?"

"Rivka . . ." He was becoming exasperated.

"No, extra money is fine, but not that way. So we won't be millionaires. We'll manage."

"Unless I make extra money, you can say good-bye to that apartment we want some day," he said brusquely.

"We have a roof over our heads, and food. And maybe the apartment will come. Who knows?" She smiled a little. "Maybe they'll publish my thesis, and I'll become a best-selling author."

Noise came from the classroom, and they both looked in. Children were scrambling around. A pencil and a spit wad sailed through the air.

"I've got to get back," she said, taking his arm.

"I can see."

"But I'm fixing you a wonderful dinner tonight. Chicken the way you like it."

"Me."

"For you and Papa. It'll make everything nice for you two. I'll have it all ready. All you have to do is shove it in the oven, heat it, and eat it."

"Me and Papa."

"You understand, okay?"

He gave her a wry smile. "I'm getting good at it. Or at least used to it."

"Please, what can I do?" She smiled apologetically. "I've got the Weisenthal lecture at seven."

"I'll be sure and wear an apron."

"Stop it." She gave him a quick peck on the cheek, reached for the door, then stopped, licking her lips. "What's that taste, on your face?"

"Show business."

"You paint yourself?"

"I'll tell you about it later."

"I don't think I want to know."

"That's . . ." she closed the door behind her, leaving him to finish the sentence for himself only, "part of the trouble."

He had started for the stairs when he saw Rabbi Birnbaum standing in the doorway to his office, his hands clasped over his belly. The rabbi was not as old as he looked. Like many of the men in the congregation, he seemed to encourage signs of advancing age as if in a race with the end of the neighborhood.

"Hello, Rabbi."

The rabbi nodded, with a look suggesting that what he saw was as disagreeable as he expected.

"I know I look a mess, Rabbi, not shaved and all. I'm sorry."

"Yussel . . ." He paused, considering his words. "We have to talk."

"I'm kind of in a rush, Rabbi. Can it wait?"

The rabbi shrugged. "Young people, a rush is what their lives are about. I'm not talking about a half-hour sermon. But important, I think. I'm getting complaints, Yussel." The rabbi cleared his throat and nodded.

Jess liked Rabbi Birnbaum. He was quiet and

wise, a steady influence on the congregation, with a
keen ear for politics and a firm conviction in his
mission. But they were a small world apart.

"The music you want to sing on Shavuos," the
rabbi went on, a bit gloomily, "it's too . . . too . . ."

"Lively?"

The rabbi held up his palms. "It's a celebration,
yes. After all, God didn't pass the Ten Commandments
to Moses on Mount Sinai so we could hold a funeral.
But lively, not lively—that's not the point. But it's not
right, the music. You know right. You have to face it,
Yussel. Keep in mind," he raised an index finger,
"what's right for you may not be right for us—for all
of us. We are not children scattered to the winds, each
to go his own way—you understand me, Yussel? We
are a congregation. And what you have to face is that
the music should—"

"Later, Rabbi, okay?" Jess smiled as graciously
as possible. "Right now I have to face a different kind
of music."

"Ah . . ." The rabbi tilted up his head in both
understanding and resignation.

"And that's not right either," Jess said more softly as he trotted up the stairs.

It was warm outside the synagogue. The poor
little tree's few new leaves fluttered hopefully in the
breeze. He crossed the street to the small apartment
house, whose soot-darkened brick walls were patched
with cracked plaster. A group of garbage cans leaned
together on the sidewalk like drunks, their tops tilted
at odd angles.

Jess stooped to pick up one of the tops that had
fallen off, and he heard the sound of single notes being
picked out on a piano. He looked up to the third floor,
their apartment, where the sound was coming from the
open window, where lace curtains moved gently as if
dancing to the music.

He smiled to himself and went up.

He opened the door quietly and stepped in, closing it as quietly behind him. Across the living room,
near the open window, the cantor was seated at the
small upright, with one finger plunking out the melody

of a religious song, then pausing to mark the sheet music in front of him with a pencil.

He watched his father for a few moments, feeling a mix of pride for the man's unfailing dignity and sorrow for the man's relatively dismal surroundings: a small apartment with two tiny bedrooms, a living room, a kitchenette; faded light blue paint peeling from the ceiling; linoleum floor on which was a worn brown rug. It was his father's home, as well as his own and Rivka's. "Convenient," his father would say with a shrug, "just across the street from the shul, and nothing to complain about."

His back to the door, the cantor didn't see Jess enter. But quickly he sensed his presence, and showed it only by a slight hitch in his playing and marking. He continued as Jess walked softly over.

"Papa . . ."

"Welcome home." His father didn't look at him.

"Papa, I want to explain about last night."

He continued picking out notes. "So explain." His tone was calm, not unkind. "When I called the jail this morning, they had no Yussel Rabinovitch. Only a Jess Robin." Now he turned to Jess. "So why a Robin?"

Jess gazed into his father's sadly inquiring eyes. "A robin sings," he said weakly.

"A Rabinovitch sings." The cantor spoke quietly, evenly. "For five generations a Rabinovitch sings. In the synagogue."

"I sing in the synagogue."

"It's true. As a Rabinovitch, you sing. Sometimes. Sometimes a little late. An assistant cantor, you come and go, sometimes sing."

"Papa, I love to sing." He took a step closer and put a hand on the sheet music. "But as poor as the synagogue is, I know they can't afford to pay me any more than they do."

"It's true, we aren't wealthy."

"So if Rivka and I are ever going to have our own place, I have to pick up some extra money where I can. By singing. Papa," he leaned over to look at him, "what's so terrible?"

"You ask me? If it's not so terrible, why the sneaking around?"

"Because *you* think it's terrible."

"Terrible I don't know. It is not right." His father looked away. He put his hands on his thighs for a moment, then got up and went over to the window and pushed the curtains open a bit wider, letting more light into the room. "God gave you your voice for His use—not yours." He stood with his back to Jess, gazing out the window. "Your voice belongs to God."

"God doesn't pay so good."

Instantly Jess regretted his impulsive sardonicism, and the old man stiffened as if shot.

He turned slowly to Jess, eyes quivering behind his glasses. "What?"

"I didn't mean—"

"He doesn't pay so good?" The cantor's strong voice trembled. "God doesn't pay enough money for your services? For giving you life, He should pay a union wage?"

"No . . ."

"When the bullets were flying in the streets, and He saved your life—you were in His hands, and He could have taken you, but He saved you. For what? For this? To hear *this?*"

His father's fists shook at his sides, his gray hair quivered on his head. His voice rose. "To hear you say He doesn't pay so good? Is that why He saved you?"

"Papa, please—"

His face and voice were fierce now, one fist was raised. "I hear you, *He* hears you. Pay so good! What you owe to God you can never pay back. Never!"

The old man's body drooped, he was suddenly spent. It was as if the words had taken everything from him, drained him in an instant, leaving him a hollow sack of clothes about to fall under their own weight.

Jess ran to him, threw his arms around him, hugged him. "I'm sorry, Papa," he mumbled, his mouth buried in his father's shoulder. "I didn't mean it, I shouldn't have said it. It wasn't what I mean, what I think. I'm so stupid sometimes."

His father's knees buckled slightly, and Jess helped him to the easy chair facing the window and lowered him gently into the seat.

"Can I get you something, Papa?" He smoothed his father's hair with his hand. "Some tea, Papa? A little schnapps? Might help you relax, feel better."

His father waved weakly no; he just sat there, taking some deep breaths, blinking, recovering.

Jess went out to the kitchen anyway and put the teakettle on the burner.

He came back to see his father sitting more erect, breathing evenly, his eyes returning to their normal warm luster. "Papa, I'm really sorry. I really am."

The cantor pursed his lips, narrowed his eyes briefly, then slowly nodded. "I know you are, Yussel. I know you are sorry. You say things too quickly, and sometimes you don't mean them. Sometimes, though, they are a hint of what's in your heart."

"Not this time, Papa. Not about God. The money, you know, sometimes I think about that. But the other things—"

"I understand you better than you think, my son. After all, didn't I raise you? Teach you what I could? Listen? Watch? Yes, I understand. But Yussel, it can't always be your way."

"Of course not, Papa."

His father shook his head impatiently. "The rabbi told me he's getting complaints. It hurts. Because he cares about you. Maybe he doesn't understand you like I do, but he cares. Not just about you. The whole congregation, he must care about. So the complaints. You want to change this, you want to change that. You want things ... modernized. Eh?" He raised his eyebrows. "You want to put more prayers into English."

"All right, Papa." Jess knelt in front of him. "Not now."

"Yes. Now. Later is not better. And new is not always better. That's what I'm talking about. It is the irony with those like you who are so anxious to change things and so reluctant to face the issues of such change now, before it occurs. Much is changing

around us, some good, some bad, but changing,
whether we like it or not. But traditions, some of them,
we hold on to because they give us a foundation, hold
us together, unite us. Some things it's more important
not to change."

"Even when they're wrong?"

"Who says they're wrong?" The cantor narrowed
his eyes, his voice grew deeper, more firm. "You?" He
put his knuckles on his knees. "Assistant Cantor Yussel Rabinovitch? Is that who says what's right and
what's wrong?" His voice softened again, and he
leaned back and knitted his fingers together. "So much
is changing so fast. So much. Let there be something
that's just the way it always was." His eyes were nearly
closed, he seemed to be speaking almost to himself.
"The way it always was. So you know where you
stand, what you can depend on. Some few things to
which we can be true, things true to us."

The teakettle whistled.

"All right," Jess said, tapping his father's knee
and rising, "okay." He started to turn away. "Let me,
just get—"

His father suddenly raised a hand, commanding
his attention. "Those of us who survived," he pro-
ceeded in low, authoritative tones, "why did we survive? Why us? Those of us fortunate enough to be
chosen for survival, what would be our purpose? His
purpose? Did we survive just to get rid of everything
we knew? To change all our ways? Then why did we
survive at all?" His eyes took on a faraway look,
piercing right through Jess. "Let Hitler win, then, finally."

Jess studied the old man, seeing the strength mus-
tered in him, the qualities of survival, the pain of it.

"*He* couldn't wipe us out," his father said, shaking a finger. "No. For all his changes, for all his armies
and machines and camps and gases, he could not wipe
us out. Now," abruptly his gaze focused on Jess, directly, intimately, "you want *us* to wipe ourselves out?
You want *us* to do the job no Hitler could do? Such
a simple thing, you think, a prayer. Why say it one
way when we could say it another? Why believe

one way when we could believe another? Ah, Yussel, this: people were killed for saying a prayer a certain way. Our people. Yes? Then it was our enemies themselves who testified to the importance of it. Important enough to kill to change us, or to eradicate us forever."

He pushed himself erect and brushed by Jess to take the center of the room. "Those thousands, millions, died. Fathers, sons, mothers, daughters. For believing a certain way, for praying a certain way. We owe it to them to keep saying it their way. That is our debt which we gladly bear. That's why God spared us. To carry on the traditions of our people. A simple prayer?"

He gave Jess a knowing nod, then a cursory wave of the hand. "You think it's an accident you can sing? Somebody said, eeny, meeny, miney, mo, let this one sing?"

"No, Papa." A frog in his throat made the words squeak.

"If you're a Rabinovitch, you're a cantor. That's why you can sing. And lucky you can. A gift for which you were chosen."

He smiled briefly, lightening the tone, causing Jess to sag in resignation.

"That's why it's so wrong for you to do all this other craziness," his father went on in a more moderate but no less firm manner. "No, my sweet, angry young boy, you can't turn your back on what has always been. It is with you, with all of us. Some new ways are good, you take them on. But the past you have with you, in you, and you keep that which is good, which is true. The past, that's where you come from, how you know who you are. And if you don't know where you come from, how can you know where you're going?"

"Okay, Papa," Jess sighed, "okay."

"Okay?" His father's arched eyebrows demanded more. "Okay?"

"Okay, I know who I am and where I come from and what I have to do."

"So?"

"I'm an assistant cantor who has to go in there," he hooked a thumb toward the bathroom, "and shave, and change the music back for Shavuos and do everything to make everyone happy."

His father smiled. "You think you can do everything to make everyone happy?"

"No."

"A little, you can do."

"Yes."

"Your part, as I try to do mine."

"Yes."

"So?" His father spread his arms grandly. "In your own words, Yussel—what's so terrible?"

"I'll make the tea."

Jess stirred when Rivka came to bed and, half awake, put his arm around her. He awakened fully with the minor disappointment of feeling her cotton nightgown, rather than her skin. He had gone to bed naked, waited for her as long as he could keep his eyes open before the effects of the long, sleepless night in jail overcame him.

She had her back to him. He tugged her gently but she didn't move. He slid against her, forming himself to her, his knees tucked into the backs of hers.

"I'm sorry I woke you," she said softly. "I tried to be quiet."

"I waited for you."

"I stayed a little late. A bunch of us talked with Dr. Weisenthal after. Go to sleep." She reached behind her to tap his side. "You need your sleep."

"I need you." He pressed himself against her, found her large, soft breasts with his hand, and traced her form from them down along her waist and hip.

"Did you straighten things out with Papa?"

"Yes."

"Good. Good night, Yussel."

"Riv . . ."

"It's so late. We both need our sleep."

"But we haven't, not since Sunday we haven't—"

"You count days? Like we have a schedule?"

"It's important to me, to have you. I waited, thinking about you."

"Thinking about me? Or that?"

"Both."

She was quiet for a moment as he stroked her. "Maybe I waited for you last night."

He withdrew his hand irritably. "Like I didn't want to be home, like jail was a night on the town."

"Well, that's what happens."

"Meaning just exactly what?"

Still she remained immobile. "When you go and do those things."

"Sing to make some extra money."

"In that kind of place."

"Extra money for us!"

"Not for me, that kind of money."

"And so this is my punishment?"

"Just when it's convenient for you, it's not always convenient for me."

"It's important."

"Maybe too important for you, Yussel. When you hang around people like that, places like that, the kind of dirt that goes on, what gets into your mind . . ."

"Shit."

"Oh, that's nice, Yussel."

"But Riv," his tone softened, became more pleading, "I have my music, just like you have your studies."

"So we're both very busy."

"Does that mean there isn't any time for love?"

Now she rolled away from him, onto her back. "Don't we love each other, all the time?"

"But doesn't that include—"

"Bickering doesn't help anything."

"No."

"Some things should just be natural, Yussel, not forced."

"Okay."

"So," she put two fingers to his lips, a kind of kiss, "good night."

"Night."

But he lay awake a long time, trying to understand, trying not to be angry, not being fully successful with either.

The drab confines of the small synagogue had been transformed by gay decorations of greenery and fruits befitting the festival of Shavuos, and the stark wooden benches, so often nearly empty, were today filled by the full congregation.

Nor were the faces somber. They reflected not only the celebrative time but also the pleasure from the focus of their attention.

Jess, in full cantorial robes and poised regally, was singing alone the final, lilting hallel psalm of the service. His baritone flowed with apparently effortless power and range, flooding the temple with further beauty and spirit, causing the congregation to sway with him in rhythmic captivity. It was one of those rare times when, as members of the congregation would put it, "Yussel really sings for us."

Off to the side, his father and Rabbi Birnbaum swayed too, his father with closed eyes and smile almost audible like a cat's purr.

Jess, without looking at the faces, sensed the audience and his command of it. When he finished, giving a slight deferential bow of the head, there was a rustling of approval throughout the room that stopped on the verge of outright applause.

The service ended, Jess was pleased and satisfied. He was doubly warmed by the pat on the back from his proudly smiling father.

"It was beautiful, Yussel," the cantor said as the congregation milled toward the exit, "beautiful." He winked. "You'll be taking my job away sooner than I wish if I'm not careful. A young voice like yours, the power, the excitement, the range—I have to recognize that while you will get better and better, I will not."

"You sing magnificently, Papa. There are things you do with the prayers, touches you have, an appreciation that I doubt I'll ever reach."

"Appreciation. Ah, there are things an old cantor appreciates, like still being able to sing, it's enough to appreciate. And of course to be of service to the shul.

These are things that come. Mortality, my son, makes an old cantor like me appreciate." He looked at his watch, holding the dial between his fingers and adjusting the distance to his eyes. "Almost twelve." He sighed. "Wouldn't you know it—the day of the big reunion and I've got to be in three places at the same time. Mr. Guttenberg is giving a luncheon, Mrs. Siegel is giving a tea, and Mr. Abramowitz is giving a donation. What time is everybody coming?"

"If you're back by four, Papa, you won't miss a thing. I'm glad you liked my singing today."

"Liked? Ah, my young son, like is what some unrelated cantor or rabbi might express, love is what a father does." He smiled and looked off. "It'll be so good to see them all again."

"I'm sure they all look forward just as much to seeing you."

He winked. "I might even dance with Mrs. Sugarman." He lowered his voice. "I just hope she hasn't put on any more weight." He dismissed the thought with an airy wave. "Well, look, I'm already dressed up." He pulled open his robe to reveal his black suit. "I'll rush through everything and be there as soon as I can." He started off, saying over his shoulder, "You can start without me, but don't enjoy yourself until I get there."

"Promise." Jess smiled fondly after his father, feeling the sweat dribble itchily from his armpits, making him wish he could scratch. He had put a lot into it after all.

"Very nice today, Yussel." Rabbi Birnbaum smiled beneficently. "A bit more—uh—bouncy than is perhaps traditional, but very nice." He put on a mock-stern expression and waggled a finger. "You see, Yussel? You can do it the right way when you want to, and you see how much it is appreciated."

Jess smiled coolly and cleared his throat. "I'm glad it was appreciated, Rabbi. But what you really mean is, I can do it *your* way when I want to."

Rabbi Birnbaum maintained his smile, striking a paternal pose with his hands clasped over his belly. "You don't think it was right?"

"Well . . ." Jess hadn't meant to get into this, and squirmed uncomfortably with the moisture under his arms.

"It is a thing with the young, Yussel, sometimes to think a thing is wrong because it is a thing believed in by old people. But that is simplistic. Right is not a difference between young and old. And you are not so simplistic as to think so."

"No, I hope not."

"It is not wrong for the young to question, Yussel."

"I'm glad you feel that way."

"Just so you listen as well. Neither are the old wrong for believing in traditions."

"Nothing is automatically right or wrong."

The rabbi chuckled from deep in his belly. "Nothing is automatic in anything at all, my fine young cantor."

"Excuse me," said Tillie Lev, stepping tentatively to the dais. She served as a sort of secretary. "Excuse me for interrupting, Rabbi Birnbaum. Yussel, there is a call for you in the office. I think it's long-distance."

"Really? Excuse me, Rabbi."

"May it be good news."

Jess headed down the hall for the office, puzzled by his happy reaction to a long-distance call, since he never got any good news that way. He passed the social hall where people were busy decorating for the reunion.

He paused before picking up the receiver. Long-distance could be just New Jersey, after all. Maybe an old friend wanted a place to spend the night. "Hello?"

"Hey, hey, hey!" came the happy voice.

"Who's this?"

"For a man with such a fine ear, you sure got a short memory."

"Bubba!" Jess slapped his thigh.

"Bates, in case you forgot the last name too, white boy."

"Bubba! How the hell you been? How's Los Angeles? What the hell's happening? What are you—"

"Sit down, my man."

Jess stood for a second, blinking, then hurried around the desk and sat in the swivel chair. "Okay, I'm sitting down."

"Are you listening carefully?"

"Come on, Bubba, you're driving me nuts!"

"We got a gig out here, a big one."

"How big?"

"Lennox. We're backing him up on an album session, the Brothers Four."

"Bubba, that's sensational! Congratulations! How did you—"

"I ain't finished, if you got a minute."

"There's more?"

"A little. You know how hot Lennox is."

"Of course. Top of the charts."

"And you know he's crazy."

"Yeah, but who cares? Long as you got the—"

"You know *how* crazy?"

"You tell me."

"I just happened to show him some of your songs. That's how crazy *I* am. And those songs, that's what he wants to record. That's how crazy *he* is."

Jess slapped a hand to his forehead and moved his lips soundlessly.

"You still there, my man?"

"I'm here. Bubba, I'm here. I'm just stunned. I don't believe it."

"Believe it. He wants your ass out here, right away."

"Bubba, you're just gonna have to talk to me. I can't do anything but listen right now. I can't believe it. You talk. Fill me in. Let me breathe."

"Okay, I'll run it down for you . . ."

Jess bolted out of the synagogue, slithered through a bunch of departing worshipers, bumping shoulders and saying "Excuse me . . ." plunged across the street, oblivious to the screeching brakes of a delivery van and the driver's shout of "Idiot punk!"

He raced up the stairs and burst into his apartment, calling "Rivka! Rivka!"

Rivka lurched back from the dining table she was using for a desk, her eyes wide with fright, her mouth open.

"Sorry." He tried to calm down, waited to catch his breath, while he smiled to ease her shock at his explosive entrance. "I just got . . . something to . . . tell you," he said between gasps.

"Oh." She held up a hand. "Just a minute. I'm right in the middle of a sentence." She returned to typing notes from a yellow pad. Reference books, some open, some closed, were spread around the table, along with several loose pages, a half-filled coffee cup.

"I gotta tell you."

"Okay, okay, one second. I don't want to forget." She finished the line she was typing, leaned back, and looked up.

"Bubba just called. From L.A. The guys are doing backup for Keith Lennox. You know who he is?"

She nodded, bent back over her typewriter, and pecked out a few words.

"Bubba showed him some of my songs, and Lennox wants to record them."

She stopped again and looked up, not smiling.

"But that's only part of it. Lennox wants me to come out to the Coast for two weeks to work on the songs with him."

"The rock-and-roll singer and dope addict."

"He's not a dope addict, Rivka, come on, you think they're all dope addicts." Some of the excitement quickly drained from him. "He's a top singer, and he wants me to work with him on my songs. Don't you understand?"

Her expression didn't change. "What did you tell him?"

"What did I tell him? What did I *tell* him! He's going to pay me two thousand dollars! *Two big ones!* Plus royalties on the album. You know damn well what I told him."

She stared at him curiously. "I've never seen you so excited about anything."

"I've never *been* so excited about anything. Riv,

two grand for two weeks. We can get our own place. We can have a kid. Our own life."

"That simple."

"It's a break. I've been playing for a break. It's for *us,* Riv."

"Suddenly you want a child."

"Riv, Riv," he put an arm lightly around her shoulders, "I've always wanted one. Just not here, not in this kind of place, not when we couldn't afford it."

"You think that's all that matters?"

He stepped back and looked at her. "What's the matter, Riv?"

She shrugged and put her hands on the typewriter keys without typing anything. "I want to finish my work, get my degree, and, yes, have a family. I want a normal life."

"And this is a way we can get it!"

"By going to Hollywood to work with a rock-and-roll musician."

"L.A., for two weeks."

She narrowed her eyes to look at him. "You sure that's all?"

"What do you mean?"

"You don't have any funny ideas, do you?"

"What do you mean? What kind of funny ideas?"

"Funny funny."

"You gotta explain yourself, Rivka, I don't know what you're talking about."

"I don't know. Messing around with that kind of life. Like some kind of magic solution to everything. With those people, doing that kind of stuff, with whatever comes with it, what it does to you . . ."

"Rivvie," he put his arm around her again, more firmly this time, "I know who I am. I'm an assistant cantor. I know where I come from and where I'm going. I'm not going to change. In two weeks, I'll be coming back from Los Angeles to New York. And— oh, God! I forgot the main part. You're going too!"

"Me?"

"They're paying for everything—plane fare, a place to stay—and we can—"

"How can I leave?" She got up, letting his arm fall from her shoulders, and went over to the window. She spoke softly. "I've got my job at the school. I've got to finish my thesis."

"But, but those things are—"

"Important. They are very important to me. Especially my thesis. I don't think you understand how much that means to me."

"I do. I really do. I just thought it wouldn't hurt to have it delayed a little."

"No, I can't do that. And . . ." her voice became even softer as she looked at him, "I don't want you to go either."

There was suddenly a distance between them that he didn't understand, as if she were speaking from the other side of a chasm. "Why not?"

"I don't know." She turned away toward the window. "I'm afraid." As if to protect herself, she pulled the curtains closed.

So thrilled and excited a few minutes before, Jess now felt resentment creeping up on him, familiar resentment that he tried to suppress. In his disappointment, it stalked him like a cat after an unwary squirrel. "You're always afraid lately," he said as evenly as he could, moving over to the table. "Ever since you started working on this thing." He gave a backhand slap to the white page in the typewriter. "This damn thing is making you afraid."

She leaned back against the wall and folded her arms, facing him. "I was afraid long before that," she said quietly.

He snatched up the title page from the stack of typed pages and spouted what he read. "Concentration camps! The survivors! The effect on their children! What is this, Rivka, your doctoral thesis or your diary?"

"A little of both. Please don't wrinkle it."

He wanted to control himself, and did, to a degree. But it was as if the past were forever gnawing at them—not even their own past, but a past for which they had no responsibility, in which they had not participated. It was all around them, in the synagogue, in the apartment, in the family.

He went over to her at the window but did not touch her. "What are you going to be? Doctor of human guilt?"

She looked at him steadily for a moment, disappointment filling her own eyes as his were filled. Then she walked past him back to the table and stood looking down at her work. "It's helping me. I know you don't like to talk about it, but it's helping me understand."

"Us, I was thinking about."

"Well, each of us has to deal with what's inside. And there is something in me, some nameless thing. I can't explain it well. But somehow, if I can take this feeling and wrap it in a word, a black-and-white word, it somehow doesn't seem so frightening anymore. It becomes just a word, you know? It's like I take it out of my gut and put it on paper." She made claws of her hands and drew them across her midsection and then extended them toward the table. "And then it's just a word, not so much a horrible feeling." She picked up a sheet of notes. "Here. I'm looking at the word right now." She traced her finger under it. *"Differentness.* There is nothing wrong with that word. But as a feeling," she turned to him, "why should that scare the absolute life out of me?"

"I don't know. I'm not an intellectual like you."

"It's not intellectual, Yussel. It's feelings I'm talking about. Feelings that I'm trying to work out with my thesis. It shouldn't bother you that I'm working like this, that I'm going for a doctoral thesis. That doesn't make me smarter or anything. I'm just trying to deal with things that are bothering me, and make something out of myself, something worthwhile." She, added wryly, "I can't sing, you know."

"Come on, Riv," he crossed to her, "you know I'm proud of you. It's just that I don't have your fears, Rivka. I'm not afraid."

"Nothing worries you?"

"Sure, of course I have worries, money worries,

worries about my music. But I don't have fears like you. I'm not living in the past."

"Sitting here at the typewriter, day after day, organizing my feelings and facts for a thesis that makes sense today—that's living in the past?"

"It's not just that, you know what I mean. But your subject, your concerns—the war is over, Rivka."

"Some struggles continue."

He sighed in exasperation. "Well, I have my own wars to fight, then, if that's what we call them." He fixed her with a stern gaze. "I'm going, Rivka. With you or without you, that's your choice. But I'm going."

She nodded and said evenly, "When will you tell Papa?"

"Today. At the party."

"At the party, the celebration, that's when you'll tell him."

"Why wait? He might as well know. It's not that big a deal."

"It's his reunion day with the others. Can't you wait? You don't have to spoil it for him."

"You don't have to spoil it for me either, Rivka."

"I didn't mean to. I'm just telling you the truth."

"That you're afraid."

She hesitated. "Yes."

"But when I come back with the money, then you won't be afraid."

Without answering, she sat down and resumed typing.

Chapter 3

"Do you ever wish you weren't Jewish?" Rivka asked, coming out of the bathroom nicely dressed in blue, her curly black hair shiny, her lips tastefully glossed, a hint of color added to her cheeks.

"No, why?"

The earlier tension between them had faded; she had typed awhile and then come and given him a hug. And while they hadn't discussed anything further, they were more comfortable together as they prepared for the festivities over at the social hall of the synagogue. And her question to him carried no more than a tone of curiosity.

"Oh, I don't know. A lot of people wish they weren't, sometimes."

"You think my flowered tie is wrong?"

"Not at all. It matches the season."

He straightened his tie in front of the mirror. "You think I wish I wasn't Jewish sometimes?"

"Well, there's Jewish and there's Jewish, you know?"

"If you're talking Orthodox, I'm not orthodox about much of anything, I guess."

"But you don't mind being . . . different."

"Rivka." He came over and took her by the shoulders. "Why don't you ease off that, hunh? You're just going to drive yourself crazy. We're not all that different—not you and I, at least."

"We'd better get going."

The social hall was colorful and loud. Families

41

ranging in generation from small children to grandparents, with even a smattering of great-grandparents, sat at tables or milled around, eating, drinking, and dancing. Central to the noise and color was the strolling six-piece band, dressed in plaid jackets and large black bow ties, that serenaded the hall and propelled the dancers with its driving beat of klezmer folk songs.

"So," Jess said as they entered, leaning close to Rivka's ear to be heard over the happy din and the music, "some good Jewish jazz. Listen to that trumpet player. He's good, Rivka."

They worked their way in among the tables and sat down, waving to people and mouthing hellos that could barely be heard.

Jess scanned the hall, then slapped the top of his head. "Will you look at Papa!"

"Where?" She leaned toward him, trying to follow his look.

"Right out in the middle, dancing with Mrs. Sugarman!"

Rivka put a hand over her mouth to conceal her giggle. Then she said, "He's enjoying himself, it looks like."

"But what a load. She must have put on fifty pounds."

"You shouldn't talk so loud."

The cantor spun the large woman around the floor with surprising lightness, both of them smiling broadly, wagging their shoulders to the rhythm.

Jess kept his eyes on his father, enjoying the sight of the man engaged in such a youthful dance, so obviously pleased with himself.

Rivka looked around, nudged Jess, and shook her head. "Look at all the old people. They're amazing, aren't they? So happy."

"Why not? The place is a madhouse."

"But it's hard to believe they came out of the concentration camps half dead."

"Rivka!" He slapped her thigh playfully. "Give it a rest—give *yourself* a rest. You're not doing research here."

The cantor danced close by, giving Jess a gay

wave that included Mrs. Sugarman's hand in his own. Jess waved back.

"Your father's having a wonderful time," Rivka said.

"He sure is. I love it."

"It's a shame you have to tell him today."

"Rivka," he said seriously, "let's just have a good time ourselves for a while, okay? Don't always put a sad light on everything. Everybody's having a good time."

"But sooner or later today you're going to tell him, and then he won't be having such a good time. It's too bad it can't wait."

"But I'm leaving first thing in the morning. You want me to wake him up at dawn and tell him just before I run out the door? I *have* to tell him today."

"There's Uncle Leo," she said, motioning toward a table near the wall. "He's not dancing."

"He looks like he *has* been dancing, see?"

Leo was mopping sweat from his brow and neck with a handkerchief hidden as discreetly as possible in his hand.

Jess watched his father engineer Mrs. Sugarman off to her table, pull the chair out for her gallantly, let her ease herself into it, then bow gracefully before starting over to them.

Jess said, "Rivka, you want to dance?"

"Sure."

"Wait a sec." He left and slithered quickly through the crowd to Uncle Leo's table. "Leo, how about dancing with my wife?"

"Shalom, Jess. You sang so well today."

"Thanks. Dance with Rivka?"

"I'm resting." Leo drooped his shoulders for emphasis.

Jess put a hand under his arm. "You're dancing."

Leo gave a resigned shrug and slowly rose. "I'm dancing."

Jess led him back, took Rivka's arm to help her up, and aimed the two together. "Show time," he said, causing Rivka to wince.

As she went off with Leo, she looked back at Jess, unsmiling.

Jess groaned inwardly. He wasn't looking forward to what he had to do any more than she was.

The cantor arrived, plopped into Rivka's chair, and sighed wearily.

"How you doing, Papa?" Jess clapped him on the back.

"Oy, Mrs. Sugarman has put on forty pounds—twenty on each foot."

"I was off by ten pounds."

They laughed together. The cantor watched the dancers. A faint smile came over his lips and seemed to freeze there. It was a smile familiar to Jess, and he braced himself for what he expected, what came.

"I used to dance all the time with your mother," his father said in a matter-of-fact tone, at once reflective and mechanical. "How she loved to dance. How she loved music, your mother. It made her spirits soar. She could make anything okay, with music. It was in her soul."

"It's in all our souls, Papa," Jess said, trying to change the course of the conversation.

His father laughed lightly, nodding, still looking off at the dancers, but Jess thought not seeing them. "In the displaced persons camp after the war, she found a record—what was it?—an American record. She found it in a pile of things, no cover on it, not badly scratched, not even warped. The mood something. Something about a mood." His father knitted his brows severely, trying to remember.

" 'In the Mood,' " Jess said.

"That's it, that's the one. 'In the Mood.' " Now he looked at Jess and hummed the opening strains—not quite the right rhythm, not quite the right melody. There was no buoyancy in his father's voice. It was more like a chant.

He went on. "I remember when you'd cry and she'd sing you to sleep. No lullaby, she would sing a real song. 'In the Mood.' " He resumed his humming.

"I know, Papa." Jess didn't like interrupting his father's reverie, but neither did he think his father really enjoyed the recollections. It was more like pain he once in a while felt compelled to put himself through, often when he had been enjoying himself. "It's a nice song. I always liked the song. Papa—"

"Then in Eretz Yisroel, she found a new favorite song. The one they always danced to in the Kibbutz. It became *her* song. Nobody could dance to it with such spirit as she. She was always the leader. Yes ..." he paused. "Dancing like crazy, and always coming back red in the face. Such spirit. Such joy! What music meant. Nobody got more from it. Everybody knew ..."

Jess waited for him to continue, wanting him to stop, not wanting to interrupt, yet waiting for an appropriate break. Now it became important for him to tell his father his news if only to break the spell of those awful memories.

When his father remained silent, Jess said, "Yes, Papa. You've told me about it many times."

"It is good to know, good to remember."

"Well, it's ... yes. Papa, I have something to tell you—"

"Then that day," the cantor suddenly resumed, in a slower, much more somber voice, "that awful day ..."

"Papa."

He looked far off, and his hand rose a few inches off the table and fanned slowly, as if tracing the scene. "You were playing in the street with the other children. And they came from the beach ..." There was a hitch in his voice, and it became husky. "With their guns, they came ..."

"I know, Papa." Jess touched his sleeve, hoping to rouse him from this dreadful, dreamlike recitation.

"They started shooting." His voice firmed, he fairly spat the words. "Shooting! Not aiming at anything. Just shooting. At the children, at anything. Your mother came running out, and the bullets found her ..."

"Papa, stop!"

His father froze, then sagged in his chair.

The music had stopped for a break. The dancers,

flushed and panting, fanned out to their tables to rest. Chatter and laughter took over the room.

Jess put a hand over his father's. "Hey, Papa," he said softly, "this is a reunion. A reunion remembers the good times. It's too happy a day to be sad. Be happy with me. Let's enjoy. Let's get some people over to our table. Who would you like to talk to? I'll get them."

Just then the klezmer band came over to their table. The leader leaned down, fingering his trumpet in front of him. "So, Cantor?" He smiled broadly. "For you, what'll it be? A special for you. Anything, we can play. What'll it be, Cantor? Czardas, polka, kazotsky? For your table, you name it."

The cantor blinked several times, as if waking. He looked around, then at Jess. "Yussel, sing it for me."

"What, Papa?"

"Yes, you sing it for me. The song your mother used to dance to. Sing it for me. That's what I want. With the music." He looked up at the trumpeter.

"All right, Papa." He began to sing softly and slowly: *"Hava Nagillah, Hava Nagillah, Hava Nagillah, vay nis machah . . ."*

The klezmers nodded together, lifted their instruments, and picked up the harmonies gently, matching the tempo Jess set.

The old man's face became peaceful as he deftly added his own voice.

Gradually Jess raised his voice and picked up the tempo. Like a magnet, the music from their table began to draw the attention of others around them. People rose from their tables and came over, adding their voices to the song.

Jess stood and let his voice out. A circle formed around him, and the circle swayed, clapping began, feet started to move, the whole circle moved. At once it was like a tidal wave of spirit. The circle of people were dancing. What had moments before been a soft appeal of melody from only the lips of Jess now became a grand, raucous, exuberant expression of joy.

Jess found himself swept into the circle, and he drew his father with him. Arms were linked around

waists as the circle swung and swayed and moved
sinuously, now leaving the table, now gaining strength,
now incorporating the whole room.

"*Hava Nagillah, Hava Nagillah . . .*"

The music went faster and faster, building and
building. Finally, the climactic, concluding crescendo:
"*Hoo D'Racheeem!*"

The dancers fell in upon each other, hugging and
gasping and staggering.

Gradually the clump sorted itself out, people
drifted back to their tables.

Jess sat down with his father, who was now limp
with exhaustion and red-faced and smiling.

Suddenly Jess hugged his father to him and
pressed his lips to the man's ear. "Papa, I got a job in
Los Angeles. I'll only be away two weeks."

"What is this?" His father pulled back.

"Two weeks, Papa. I've got a chance to make
some money."

"No."

"Rivvie and I can get our own place—"

"No, that's not the way."

"But Papa—"

"You won't come back." The cantor's voice was
low, but shaking as if from some hidden fright.

"What do you mean, I won't come back?"

"It's wrong, this thing, the kind of thing that
changes too much . . ."

"Papa, how can I not come back? You're here.
Rivka is here. My whole life is here."

The old man studied him through his thick
glasses. "Not if you go to California, then your whole
life is not here."

It was if he were not speaking for himself, but
were transmitting thoughts, words, from another
source, eerily, like a medium at a séance.

"Two weeks, that's all. I'll be back before you
know it. Trust me, Papa, believe me."

His father nodded, unsmiling. "Take care of
yourself."

"I will, Papa," Jess said, putting an arm around
his father to draw him close, "I will."

It was a long plane flight, providing endless fasci-
nations. "Due to technical difficulties with the projec-
tion equipment," there was no movie. But Jess enjoyed
lounging back with the earphones on and tuning to the
various channels of music, sticking with the Top 40 for
a while, then switching to country and western, laughing a little at the comedy channel, and even finding
classical music soothing for a time. And beneath him
under what were mainly clear skies, the United States
opened up with a vastness that awed him—the Great
Plains, the desert, even the Grand Canyon revealed a
scope to the country beyond what he had imagined.

From time to time his thoughts drifted back to his
father, and to Rivka. Oddly enough, his father seemed
more accepting of what he was doing. He would have
figured that Riv, who would benefit more directly
from this investment of his time, would have come
around to see the importance of the trip. But while
neither she nor his father really supported the idea, it
was Rivka who remained most disturbed by it in the
end.

It wasn't anything she could express to him exactly. She had vague fears and suspicions and doubts that
seemed to hang between them like a curtain. He didn't
like to think about how their relationship had become
somewhat strained by her working and studying so
much, and anyway that wasn't really the problem. The
problem had more to do with what she was thinking so
much about, and what she was thinking about so much
had less to do with Jess, in his own view, than with
history.

What made it difficult was that her absorption by
this ethnic and religious history caused her to doubt
him. It was as if she wanted him to be part of all that
past. He was more concerned with their present and
future as a married couple, without all that baggage
that she seemed compelled to attach to it.

Whatever it was, it wasn't something they had
been able to address satisfactorily together. She made
him feel like some kind of traitor to the cause—*deserter* was the word she actually used, though she didn't
directly call him that. She said there was a type who,

as represented through the ages, would abandon the historic and just and valid and necessary obligations of his people for the sake of convenience in a more wanton modern world, and she hated to think Jess "might be such a deserter."

He told her he wasn't deserting anything, just following his talents and abilities where they led him, for the benefit of them both, and that she just shouldn't worry so much about it.

"Everybody around here worries too much about it," he had said, innocently and meaning only to ease her mind.

To which she had replied, "That's exactly the kind of talk that worries me about you—as if you weren't part of everybody around here."

Ah, well, he didn't really feel like thinking that much about it now. They were descending toward Los Angeles, and the blue spots became an amazing number of swimming pools. Soon after that, he saw the palm trees, and was awed by such tropical sights he never thought he would see.

The sun was brilliant, blinding, when the plane touched down shortly after noon. He left the plane carrying his guitar and two shoe boxes. He retrieved his canvas suitcase from the baggage claim and tromped along what seemed like miles of corridors and through acres of bright terminal rooms.

Finally he was outside. Cars, people, trees—everything was dazzling. He blinked to adjust his eyes, and drank in the exotic, splendid sights. It was warm but very pleasant. Along with the acrid odor of jet fuel that hovered over the area there came whiffs of sweet things, pleasurable scents of perfume and flowers and greenery. It was a distinctly different world from the one he had left—*different* was a word that stuck in his thoughts from things Rivka said. But this was really different, nothing to do with historical junk and wrinkled scrolls of the Torah.

He was to be met, and looked around for the familiar head and cool stride of Bubba. He leaned out from the curb to look up and down the busy airport drive.

Suddenly he had to jump back as an old sports car, bright red where it wasn't dented and rusted, swerved over in front of him and squealed to a halt. He moved away from it to keep looking for Bubba, when a voice came from the car.

"Hey, mister singer-composer-fighter!"

Molly Oliver was at the wheel.

"Come on!" she called, throwing open the passenger door and leaning out.

He tossed his suitcase and the shoe boxes in the space behind the bucket seats and placed his guitar case more carefully on top. "You again, hunh?"

"Me again."

He stepped back briefly for a final look up and down at the palm trees. "Well, Yussel Rabinovitch," he said, "welcome to California."

"Come on."

He slid into the torn seat beside her. "I was expecting Bubba."

"Bubba's at the recording studio with Keith Lennox. I'm the welcoming committee. Disappointed?" She craned her neck to look out the driver's window, watching for a break in the traffic.

"No, why should I be?"

"You weren't my biggest fan when last I saw you."

"You weren't mine either."

"I bailed you out, didn't I?" She checked the traffic again, revving the engine.

"With money I was owed."

"So, who cares? You're here now."

"I guess so."

"What's in the shoe boxes?"

"Music. I brought some of my other songs. Maybe I can sell them."

"You already sell the shoes?"

"What's that supposed to mean?"

"Hold on, here we go!" She swerved violently into the lane of traffic, barely avoiding a collision, and accelerated rapidly enough to throw his head back.

"Wow. What kind of car is this?"

"MG-TD. Classic. Hold on." She dipped in and

out of lanes, almost sideswiping a limousine, then swung the wheel over as another car cut sharply in front of her, missing the fender by an inch. "Welcome to California!" she said gaily, her brown hair blowing in the wind.

"Something I just said myself."

They drove along wide, palm-lined boulevards whose enticing vistas were blurred by Molly's high-speed driving and rapid lane changes. Jess held on to the edge of the seat.

"So what do you think so far?" she asked.

"Big streets, fast cars."

"Place was designed for cars, the whole L.A. area. It's the only way you get around. You'll love it."

"I don't drive."

"I don't believe it." She glanced at him.

"Lot of people who grew up in New York don't drive. You don't need to drive in New York."

She gave a stage sigh. "So young, so innocent, so many things to experience."

"Somebody records my songs, that's experience enough."

"Really?" She flashed a cocky grin.

"Really. I'm as old as you, by the way, I'll bet."

"We're both spring chickens." She cackled as if to demonstrate. She didn't always drive this fast. She was excited. This was a big-time gig she managed to put together. But also, she was surprised to find how much she had looked forward to seeing him. He was refreshing. He was also, from what little she had seen and heard, a damn promising talent. "Married?"

"Why?"

"Interesting answer."

"Yes."

"Yes interesting, or yes married?"

"Yes."

She nodded thoughtfully. "Listen. Lennox takes a little getting used to, okay? He's weird, but he's a heavy talent. So just be cool and ride with it. We'll be there in a minute."

"I'm riding."

She noted his nervousness amid the traffic. "And counting seconds, right?"

"Eight, nine, ten . . ."

They both laughed.

He liked being with her. She was really a lady of the present. And everything about her said she was the type to get things done.

They were about to start. There was time for no more than a quick reunion with Bubba and the brothers.

Jess hugged them each, slapped palms. "I still can't believe any of this," he said, happily shaking his head. "He's really gonna do 'Love on the Rocks'?"

"Yeah, unh-hunh," Bubba said, fingering his guitar.

They seemed a bit subdued in their welcome of him, which Jess attributed to ordinary nervousness before a recording session. He had never been present at one before.

Molly tugged his arm and turned him to another man, a small, dark man in a dungaree leisure suit who was pacing back and forth. "This is Paul Rossini, the record producer."

"Come on," is all Rossini said, heading toward a glass booth.

Keith Lennox was a familiar face from his album covers and public appearances—tall and thin with narrow, sharp, bony features and long, scraggly blond hair. He was wearing a T-shirt that had on it the word *Gourds* in flowing script surrounded by flowers, and faded, flared jeans spangled with silver metal stars, and bright red sneakers. He seemed unable to stand still, and kept sniffing and daubing at his nose with the back of his hand.

"Keith," Rossini said, leaning into the booth, "this is Jess Robin."

"Pleased, I'm sure," Lennox said in dull, clipped British tones. "Let's go, this ain't no friggin' card party!" He pulled on his earphones and waved them out of the booth.

Rossini led Jess and Molly to seats in the control

booth. The engineer and sound man were near them, poised at the broad panel of knobs and buttons and lights. Rossini paced behind them.

Beyond the glass, out on the floor along with other musicians, Bubba and the brothers, also in earphones, arranged themselves among the microphones, amplifiers, and other electronic gear. Wires and cables snaked every which way over the floor.

Jess leaned to Molly to whisper, "I've never heard Lennox do a ballad like 'Love on the Rocks' before. Most of his stuff is so hard to—"

Molly shushed him with a finger to her lips.

Suddenly they began, a burst and clash of electronic sounds, distorted in high volume, snapping Jess erect in his seat.

Lennox bellowed into his mike, so close he looked like he was about to devour it. He danced and waved his arms. Whatever song this was, whatever melody, Jess could hear only clashing noise and a heavy, driving beat. He closed his eyes but didn't dare cover his ears.

Abruptly the music stopped. Lennox was shaking his head. Then as quickly they started over, Lennox even more frenetic, the musicians pounding to keep up with him. Sweat already bathed Bubba's face.

They stopped again.

Jess took the opportunity to whisper to Molly, "When is he going to do my song?"

"He's doing it now," Molly whispered back.

"What? What?" Jess put the tips of his fingers to his temples and said out loud, "You gotta be kidding! My song's a ballad. You can't sing it this way. He's ruining it!"

"Can it, mister," Rossini's voice growled behind him. "That's his style. That's what made him a millionaire."

"But my song, it's wrong, it's—"

"Ten Grammys, five Rolls Royces, six swimming pools—that makes him right."

The sound man squirmed in his seat. "Sounds like he's singing under one of the pools," he muttered.

Rossini spun toward him. "You don't like it, you

can walk!" Then he quickly put a hand on the man's shoulder "Don't."

"But it's wrong!" Jess persisted, appealing to Rossini. "It's too fast, too crazy. You can't understand it!"

"That's why you're here, Robin. He changed the tempo, so you gotta fix up the lyrics."

"No, it's—"

"You don't like it, *you* can walk!"

Jess started to rise, but Molly restrained him. "He can't do without the sound man," she said quietly, "but to you he didn't say 'Don't.' I told you, just be cool."

Lennox adjusted the music sheets on the stand next to the mike, signaled the control booth, and they started again.

To Jess, it was even more monstrous than before, faster, crazier.

Not that Lennox was satisfied either. He stopped suddenly again and screamed, "Cut! Cut! Cut!"

Jess felt relief. Maybe Lennox saw it wouldn't work that way.

Lennox tore off his earphones and stalked out of his booth to the band. "You apes ain't got it on!" he hollered at them, waving his arms as if he were singing. "You're draggin' me down! My soul wants to fly! Faster! Louder! Boom, boom, boom!" He swung his fist sharply up and down. "I wanna hear boom, boom, boom!"

Rossini leaned to the intercom. "We hear it okay in here, Keith," he said pleasantly.

Lennox faced the booth, flung a finger in that direction, and cried, "Then *you* make the friggin' album!" He swung his arms around, knocking over two music stands and sending sheet music fluttering like dying birds. "This crud needs all the help it can get!" He wheeled on Bubba, who stood with head lowered. "And where the hell are you? Where the hell's the lead guitar? You gotta feel that beat, ace, feel the rhythm! Ain't that supposed to be your for-*tay?*"

Bubba snapped his head up to glare at him, but held his tongue.

Lennox started away. "Maybe they ain't *all* got rhythm," he muttered.

Jess saw Bubba's hands clench on the guitar. "Mr. Rossini," he said, controlling his voice, "tell him it's a ballad. It should be sung as a ballad. That's the whole point of it."

"*You* tell him."

"Okay," Jess rose quickly, "I will."

Molly reached out for him but missed. "Jess . . . wait . . ."

"I've *been* waiting." He headed out of the booth. Cool was one thing, but how his own music was performed was quite another. He walked quickly onto the recording floor. "Mr. Lennox?"

Lennox stopped and stared at him.

"Mr. Lennox," Jess went on calmly, "I know you've got a great style, but this is really a *ballad*. You know—gentle, lyrical. Just listen to it once the right way."

Without waiting for a response, he went to the piano, motioned the pianist off the stool, and sat down. He began with the simple melody chords, then added his voice. It was bright, not draggy, but nonetheless a ballad, and, with its nice minor-chord augmentations, clearly not meant for a hard-rock rendition.

". . . Love on the rocks ain't no surprise . . ."

After a few bars, Bubba and the brothers picked up on it, filling warmly but with a firm, solid beat that pushed the song along without forcing it. The other musicians listened, nodded. Jess loved the song, more than most he had written, and was aware of the skill involved in finding just the right combination that kept such a ballad under control, strong and not drippy.

He smiled over at Lennox, sure that no serious musician could miss the point he was making, that to want to record this song at all was to want to record it right, this way—of course allowing for some differences in personal style.

But Lennox was not smiling. He glared with deepening malevolence, his lip curled into a mean snarl.

Jess let his voice out even more, trying to reach

the famous rock star by asserting the song, making him hear it.

But from the moment Jess had risen from his chair in the booth, Molly sensed it was going to go very wrong. Naturally she thought the song was beautiful, the way Jess meant it. But the gig here was to get the song recorded by a top star—a big break—and first things first. She hurried out of the booth, already knowing it was too late.

"See, Mr. Lennox?" Jess trailed off with some finishing chords and leaned back, trying to smile. "Of course we have different styles, but it's just that on this particular song—"

"You're sayin' *what?*" Lennox hissed.

"Just trying to help with—"

"You're tellin' *me?*" He jammed a thumb in his chest and his voice rose. "Tellin' everybody Keith Lennox is ruining your precious song? Me, *Keith Lennox!* You puttin' me down in front of my people?"

Jess, no longer feeling conciliatory, fought to control his temper. He didn't dare respond because he knew what his response would be.

"You answer me, punk, when I talk to you!"

Molly was frozen at the edge of the floor. Rossini pushed past her and rushed over to Lennox, grabbing his arm, patting his back.

"Hey, baby," Rossini cooed, "why you getting so excited, man? What does *he* know, hunh?" He rubbed the star's shoulder blades. "You're the king, baby, the king!"

"Friggin' right! I'm the king." Lennox never took his eyes off Jess. "No friggin' amateur who never cut a side in his life is gonna come out here and tell *me* how to do a song! Punks with advice are a dime a dozen, but they don't advise *me!*"

Jess pushed himself up from the stool. Molly scampered across the floor, holding up both hands like she was surrendering. "Stop! Please, everybody!"

Jess did stop, standing where he was by the piano. Lennox wrenched away from Rossini's grasp, took a step toward Jess, then turned back and shot a seething look at Bubba.

For a moment he stood scratching angrily at the silver stars on his pants, as if his fingers were mining for words. Then he rasped, "That's what I get for listening to a bloody bunch of niggers!"

He had barely got the words out when Jess was right behind him, spinning him around by the shoulder, and launching an overhand right.

The single punch propelled Lennox backward, crashing over music stands and amplifiers, his buckling legs becoming tangled in a web of wires as he went down.

The room for an instant was a frozen tableau, no movement, no sound.

Then Rossini said softly to Jess, "Goodbye."

"Goodbye," Jess replied just as softly. He headed for the control booth as Lennox managed to roll onto his side, lift his head, and prop himself up by an elbow.

Bubba sauntered the couple of steps to him and stood gazing coolly down, regarding the fallen star as one might a chopped vine of poison ivy. "You might as well stay right there where you are, *king.* 'Cause if you get up, you just gonna go right back down again."

Lennox lay blinking as first Bubba, then the other brothers in turn, designed their exits so as to step over him.

Molly had closed her eyes for the crucial event, missing the TKO punch but opening them to see the dreary aftermath. Avoiding the supine Keith Lennox, erstwhile financier of her latest managerial endeavor, she followed Jess to the control booth on shaky legs, taking mechanical steps, feeling woozy and swallowing what felt like a fist.

Jess scooped up his shoe boxes, hesitated, then carefully, as if donning a fine glove, slipped his fingers through the handle of the guitar case. Then he just stood, staring at the floor.

Molly leaned in the doorway, studying him. She didn't know if she felt sorry for him or not. She guessed not, because his bearing and demeanor suggested he needed no pity. She felt a little sorry for herself. But beneath it all was a subtle fascination with the volatility of this slugger from New York who could write and sing such music. She wasn't sure she should say anything. There was certainly something important to say, but she didn't know what it was. She said, "You're kind of an interesting guy, you know? You can't get through a song without belting somebody."

Jess didn't turn. He was thinking about how far from home he was, from everything. He was feeling "different." He said softly, "I don't turn the other cheek, if that's what you mean."

"So what now?"

"Home."

"You'll have to get a flight."

"I ain't gonna walk."

She nodded and pursed her lips. "Well, the bunch of us might as well go and have a beer. I know a place. You can call the airlines from there."

"No, I think I'll just—"

"Hey, bro." Bubba looked at him over Molly's shoulder. "Ain't nobody ditching nobody right this minute. Come on, we'll toss a few down. Then you can do whatever you have to do."

"Okay."

Chapter 4

They found a table near the front of the noisy little place, Donny's Do-Your-Thing Club. It was a place where the audience supplied the acts. Anyone was welcome to take the stage, and there was a mix of performances—unknown, beginning pros, energetic amateurs, outright improvisers disinhibited by a few drinks, musical acts backed up by a small, listless band. Hand-printed signs here and there on the walls said "Do Your Own Thing" and "Strut Your Stuff" and "Try It Before a Live Audience" and "There's a Bit of Show Biz In *You!*" One prominent printed placard said "Just Don't Make Us Lose Our License!"

Jess followed his friends to the table, then without sitting excused himself to go to the pay phone. He pushed his way through the crowd—mostly young people, boisterous, taunting. On the little stage, a customer was doing a comedy routine. Between the jibes and catcalls, Jess heard only one line:

"What do you call it when an accountant works at home? *Ledger-domain!*"

The crowd responded: "Boo . . . Sit down . . . Why did the chicken cross the road? . . . Give it a rest . . ."

Jess had to wait a minute before the phone was free. Then, covering one ear with his hand, he dialed American Airlines. He was put on hold. He got the number for United and dialed that. He was put on hold. He hung on for a while, dialed them both again with the same result. He didn't like being put on hold. He would keep dialing until a human being spoke to him.

At the table, Bubba and Molly ignored the performers. Timmy, Mel, and Teddy watched them.

Bubba leaned across the table to Teddy. "You gonna keep that mustache, bro?"

"Damn straight."

Their order of beers came, delivered by a harried but attractive young woman.

"Actress?" Bubba asked, looking up at her.

"How'd you know?"

"That's who waits on tables."

She sighed and nodded. "Ain't it the truth."

"So, bro," Bubba continued, "since when you wear that? We all shaved ours off just to be a little different."

"In the joint, they clip you down so close," Teddy said, "you gotta show you still got your manhood."

"Sheeiiit." Bubba laughed. "Manhood ain't fuzz on the lip. That's like old slave talk. Manhood, that's what you saw back in the recording studio, man who stands up for himself."

"Whooee, ain't that the truth!" Teddy waved his arms and widened his eyes and gave a reasonable representation of Keith Lennox's British accent. "Louder, ace! Up your ace, ace! I want boom, boom, boom!"

"And he got boom, boom, boom," Mel chimed in, swinging up a fist. "Right on the chinny-chin-chin!"

"That takes care of the manhood case," Teddy said, banging a fist on the table while they laughed.

"And the gig," Molly said. "Because you're now out of work, work, work."

"Manhood always had a price, pretty lady," Bubba said.

"I'm not in the business of managing manhood, Bubba. Musicians, I handle."

"Yeah, well—"

"But that's okay." She brightened. "I've got some great ideas."

"Better not let Jess hear 'em," Timmy said.

"Yeah, old Jess." Bubba shook his head. "He don't back down front of no man."

"That's very terrific," Molly said, "but that doesn't get his music played, much less recorded."

They drank their beer.

Bubba looked off toward the phone booth, where Jess was holding the receiver with one hand and rubbing his eyes with the other. "I tell you something, Miss Molly, I sure wish you could do something for old Jess. Come all the way out here just to get dumped on." He shook his head. "And there ain't no question that he got dumped on."

The brothers nodded.

"Us too," Teddy said. "Lennox got a foul mouth."

"What he said to us don't mean diddly," Bubba said. "The music belonged to Jess, it was his. Difference between a foul mouth and somebody messing up your music. Molly," he reached over to tap her hand, "we can't let him go home like this, just a total wipe-out. It ain't fair. Must be some kind of gig you can get him."

"Yeah. Give him some boxing gloves and a trainer. He might make a good middleweight."

"No, no, listen to me now. I'm serious. He's good, Molly. You know it. You seen he's got talent. Don't joke your way outta that. And damn, we been jivin' around with him since we were all kids. Basements, street corners, you know. You ought to see how people dig him when he cuts loose. You caught a couple minutes of it back there at the Cinderella, before the fur flew."

"Say it, bro," Mel said.

"Sorry I missed it," Teddy said.

"Stay away from other folks' wheels."

"Honest mistake. I thought it was a friend's car."

"Yeah, well, you lucky the dude didn't press charges."

"Cost me, though."

"Everything costs. You might as well take a taxi."

Jess returned to the table and squeezed his chair

in beside Molly. "I still can't get a plane. Booked solid."

"Maybe they heard about your act," Molly said dryly. There was a break in the performances, the stage was empty. Molly looked at her watch. "Well, fellas, it's been a long day, time for this old lady to split." She stuck out her hand to Jess. "If I don't see you again . . ."

Jess looked away. Molly started to get up. Bubba put a heavy hand on her shoulder and got up himself. He banged a spoon on his glass and looked around the room.

"Okay, everybody!" he shouted. "Everybody settle down!" The audience quieted some, heads turned toward him. "Listen up, everybody. We got the next act right here! I got a guy here who's gonna knock you out! One of the great belters of all time!" He added slyly, "And he can sing, too."

"Give us a break!" somebody called.

"Do it in the shower!"

"Come back Wednesday!"

"Hold it!" Bubba spread his arms. "I mean, we got an *act* here, not one of your jive fakers! Let's have a real Donny's welcome for a young man who does his own thing, man who can give you a *treat* 'stead of a treatment—from New York City, *Jess Robin!*"

Bubba started some solitary, energetic applause. He looked around from table to table, clapping harder. Little by little, other tables joined in halfheartedly.

"Get the hook ready!" somebody yelled.

Jess ducked his head. "Come on, Bubba, give me a break. Forget it." He looked cautiously around at the crowd. Somberly, he said, "I sing to God, not to a bunch of drunks."

"What you say?" Bubba challenged him. "This ain't no Saturday morning with pancakes on their heads."

Molly added a challenge of her own, a cocky smile. "A man who sings to God shouldn't be afraid of a few drunks."

Bubba picked up the applause again, and now the room was urging:

"Where's he at?"

"Louder!"

"How about 'Melancholy Baby'?"

Jess looked at Molly. The smile still played on her lips. He cocked an eyebrow. Suddenly he got up and headed for the stage.

The brothers got to their feet. "Go ahead on, Jess! . . . Do it to it!"

Bubba, applauding with the rest, elbowed Molly's shoulder. "Now you gonna see something, girl."

"Six to five it don't go the limit."

"Oh, he'll sing it. This here's *his* gig. You gonna hear what my man can *do!*"

"What do you think he'll sing?"

Bubba chortled. "Ain't no doubt in my mind, he'll do this one for Keith Lennox."

Jess borrowed a guitar from the band, thanked the man, strummed once, gave two strings some tiny adjustment, and walked hesitantly to the mike. He smiled humbly at the audience "This won't take but a minute, folks. You got anything better to do, you go right ahead. I'm just doing this for my buddies over there."

"Then why don't you do it at the table!" came one taunt.

Jess chuckled and nodded. He started with a few gentle chords as intro, then found the rhythm and began singing softly: "Where will all the time go? Time that we will never know . . ."

A few listened, most of the audience resumed talking and laughing and drinking.

But as he moved into the song, he gradually boosted his voice, the deep, husky baritone that sounded like it would come from a bigger man. " . . . Dreams may be eternity, but let them speak just silently . . ."

More and more of the audience stopped talking and turned to the stage. The hum and banter died down. Jess worked the guitar harder, more confidently, and his voice really began to roll: " . . . and never say forever anymore . . ."

Soon he had the whole audience. Molly's eyes were riveted on him. Jess felt it all—not just that the other noise died, or that the faces turned toward him—he sensed always when he was taking over.

His chords and beat became more forceful, and above the guitar rose his vocal melody, crackling with power yet flowing through the phrasing with the smoothness of a climbing and diving glider, controlled, with no strain; he could sing forever.

"... I can hear the laughter, I can hear the crying; no one needs to say a word, everything's been heard. Yes, dreams may be eternity..."

They were clapping now, with his rhythm; it began quietly and built to a wave. Over it boomed Jess's voice, reverberating off the walls. The waitresses stood still, watching and listening.

Molly was frozen in awe. Her mouth hung open. She didn't clap. She scarcely breathed. The brothers were now on their feet, swaying and snapping their fingers together as if they were part of the act, as if they had their instruments.

And finally Jess belted out the closer: "... So please don't say forever anymore!"

The place erupted. Everybody was up, cheering, raising fists, applauding. Some stood on chairs. "More! More!" came the chant.

Jess bowed again and again. The brothers yowled for encores. "Give 'em 'Don't Bother Me'!" Teddy hollered.

" 'Life and Loving You'!" bellowed Mel.

" 'Gentle Game'!" roared Timmy.

But Jess was finished. He had sung the song that had been nearly destroyed by a big star not worthy of the music. He had done it right. His audience gave him the affirmation he craved. It was enough.

He handed the guitar back to the dumbstruck band member and strode off the stage.

Bubba and the brothers continued to lead the unfading applause.

Bubba elbowed Molly again. "So what you think now, child?"

"I can't think," she said breathlessly, shaking her head.

"Just be glad he didn't catch an early flight."

"He gets on a plane now, I'll hijack it!"

"We haven't partied in a long time, bro."

"Not much to party about, Bubba," Jess said.

"Hey, you ain't gonna be down now, are you?"

"Nope. I just gotta get a flight."

" 'Cause you picked us all up tonight—ain't that right, Molly?"

"Yeah." Molly arranged trays of beer, a bottle of Scotch and one of tequila, chips, dips, olives, and pickles around her living room. The brothers dug in. "You like my place, Jess?"

"Very nice." It was a small two-bedroom bungalow, the living room furnished in contemporary style with furniture of wood and leather—or plastic—a thick white rug in the middle of the floor, small cactus plants here and there, pieces of driftwood arranged on bookcases among the books and other knickknacks, a stereo with big speakers, which Molly now turned on, and an upright piano.

"You like Charlie Parker?" she asked.

"Sure," Jess said, "who doesn't?"

"My favorite musician. If I ever have a kid, I'm gonna name him Charlie Parker."

"You gonna marry somebody named Parker?" Bubba asked.

"Well, Charlie Parker somebody."

The walls were white and had hung on them framed fabrics printed with bright abstract colors and fruit. Two hurricane lanterns and several candles lit the room cozily and sparkled off a glass cabinet on whose shelves was a mélange of framed photos large and small, including a large one of Molly in a bathing suit with a surfboard. Jess admired that shot privately and quickly, though he would have liked to study it closely. and moved over to the picture window.

The view was of the beach, and a full moon hung over the Pacific. It was a spectacular scene, full of vastness and mystery, suggesting the reaches of the world the wrong way from home. She had said they were in Venice, which he didn't know existed in California. Everything existed in California, and he struggled against the enchantment that he felt. The smooth sax of Charlie Parker in the background reinforced his mood.

The odor of a joint filled the room.

"Want a toke, hey Jess?" Teddy asked with a voice pinched to hold the breath in.

"No thanks."

"The phone's over there by the cat," Molly said.

A small black plaster cat sat poised on its haunches on an end table next to the brown sofa, and next to it was the white phone.

He dialed and asked for the next available flight to JFK, and waited while the woman worked her electronic machinery.

Molly put a glass of red wine next to him. "Kosher," she said, smiling.

"Why don't we go swimming?" Teddy said, giggling. "Let's swim to China."

"Since when can you swim?" Bubba asked.

"I'm a fish," Teddy said.

"Dead stoned trout," Mel said.

"Shark!" Teddy barked.

Jess got the information and hung up. "I got the early-bird flight," he called over to Molly. "I'll be flying at dawn."

"I'm flyin' now," Teddy said in a voice grown raspy. He was sitting cross-legged on the rug, his head tilted back, his eyes closed. "I'm the earliest bird. Me and Charlie 'Bird' Parker there."

"Minute ago you was a fish," Mel said.

"Man can be anything he wants to be. This is a free country."

"You gonna go nuts on us, Teddy?" Bubba asked, tapping him on the head with his beer bottle. "Little weed sends him right off," he said to Jess.

"Two things he thinks he can do when he gets a little high," Mel said, "swim and drive a car."

"Three!" Teddy rocked happily from side to side. "Don't forget fly!"

"Three strikes," Bubba said, "and little bro is

out." He took him under the arms and hoisted him to his feet. "I'm flyin' you home."

"Whooee!"

"Should I make some coffee?" Molly asked.

"Coffee be good," Teddy said, swaying. "And some ham and eggs, stack of cakes, tacos on the side. And a milk shake . . ."

"Thanks, Molly, but I think we just gonna cruise on out. Come on, bro."

"Little Teddy gettin' ready!" Teddy sang as the brothers moved him toward the door.

Jess followed. "Hey, maybe you guys can drop me off at the airport, hunh, Bubba? I'll just hang around till my plane leaves."

"You can hang around here," Molly said, holding the door open for the brothers. "Sack out in the extra bedroom."

"That sure sounds better than an airport bench," Bubba said.

"Well, at least I'd *be* there," Jess said.

"The airport's only ten minutes away," Molly said. "I'll drive you over." She patted Teddy on the back. "You gonna be okay?"

Teddy just grinned.

"So then, well . . ." Jess followed them a couple more steps, "so long, guys. Take it easy, huh? Thanks for everything. And, unh, I'm sorry things didn't work out so good, I mean, sorry that I—"

"Hey, my man, don't be sorry for nothing, not a damn thing. We all gonna have it together, by and by."

"Okay, well, so long, Bubba."

Bubba held out his palms. "Let's just say, later."

"Later." Jess slapped Bubba's palms lightly, watched them move off down the steps, then followed Molly back inside.

Molly went around the room gathering up plates and glasses. "So like I said, I've got the extra bedroom in there if you want to grab a few z's." She took an armload to the kitchen. "My roommate moved out a month ago. She converted to Zen."

Jess picked up more of the dishes and stood with them. "I'll sleep on the plane. I'm too wide awake now, I don't know why. What's Zen got to do with her moving out?"

"She wants the contemplative life. Simplicity, poverty, chastity—who knows? I didn't beg her to stay. A little privacy is nice too." She came back and took the dishes from him and made another trip to the kitchen. "You don't know why you're so wide awake?" she said over her shoulder.

"No."

"After singing like that, and everyone standing and cheering and treating you like a hero, a conquering hero. That's the highest high there is, Jess."

"I suppose."

"So casual. Like it happens every day." She returned with a fistful of paper towels and began wiping off the tables.

"I'm not casual. It's just, I don't know . . ."

"Homesick?" She paused and looked at him.

"Not exactly."

"Good for you. You been gone one whole day."

"Been a long day, for just one."

"I'll say. But just one is all it is." She sat back on her haunches. "Jess, why don't you stick around out here a little while? Maybe I can get you some kind of singing gig."

"I've got a singing gig. That's what I'm going back to."

"That wasn't your plan."

"Of course it was."

"I mean, what's your hurry? You were planning on a couple of weeks anyway."

"Yeah." He chuckled. "To help cut an album of my songs, I think it was. I wasn't looking for any kind of career. I'm still not."

"Maybe you should be."

"What?"

Molly had her head under the coffee table and was carefully picking up crumbs. "Maybe you *should* be looking for a career."

"I already have one, that's the point, that's what I'm telling you."

"I don't mean as some kind of church singer."

"You don't understand, Molly." Jess went over to the window and looked out at the Pacific. The moon was down, the ocean black, melting into the horizon as if there were no beginning or end to sky or sea. "A cantor is not just some church singer, like a soloist in a Methodist choir or something. He is an official in the synagogue, he leads the prayer services with his singing. And it is not just ordinary singing. It is beautiful, and some of it is very difficult. People train, like opera singers. In fact—"

"I know about cantors," Molly said, still on her knees. "Scratch a cantor and you'll find an opera singer—I've heard that. And I know about Richard Tucker and all the other famous dudes that went on to the Met or whatever to fame and glory."

"I'm not talking about fame and—"

"And I'll tell you something else that may surprise you. I've been to a synagogue. And in New York, no less. Couple guys took me. And it was one of the best, cantor-wise. The Park Avenue Synagogue. And the cantor was magnificent. Lefkowitz, his name was. You know why I got his name? Because he was one handsome and impressive dude, that's why. He was terrific, and you never know where you might find a talent, so I got his name. My friends took me there especially to hear this cantor. And the whole thing was wonderful—the organ, the choir, all of it. So you don't have to think I'm just some ignorant broad who only knows crazy rock and jazz people. I know music. And I know what you can do." She added with finality. "So."

"So you know a part of it. A different part."

"Different?"

"Our synagogue is small and simple. We don't have rich people there, with fancy doors to the ark and fancy cases for the Torahs. And we are Orthodox, really true to the traditions. We don't have a choir and organ and all that. The music is our singing, my father's and mine. I'm just the assistant cantor now."

"Your father's better than you?"

"Well, for the purposes of our synagogue, yes. And his voice? He could have been a fine tenor in an opera, I suppose. But he is a cantor. He's kind of old now, but as a cantor, he is as flawless as any I have ever heard. If I can do so well——"

"So you're a different kind of singer."

"You still don't understand." He turned to face her and leaned back against the wall. "We're a family of cantors. For five generations, there's been a Cantor Rabinovitch. My father's a cantor, his father was a cantor, his grandfather and so on."

"Rabinovitch." She put a fist thoughtfully under her chin.

"Yes. My father's name, my name. And so, after all these generations, my father's son is to be a cantor. Yussel Rabinovitch, I am the sixth generation. The tradition is terribly important."

"I can dig it." She felt a common ground between them. "My father wanted a girl. A regular girl, you know? And I'm doing the best I can." She wiped off the last end table and looked around the room, checking for anything she might have missed. "Although to hear my old man talk, you wouldn't think I was doing so hot. I've never been quite the type of girl he had in mind, never done what he's wanted me to do. Not because he wanted me to follow in his footsteps—quite the opposite. And not because I opposed him, not because he didn't love me and want the best for me. But his idea of a perfect girl, a girl headed in the right direction for a decent life, is something right out of silent movies. You cook, you sew, you get married, you give him grandchildren." She raised her eyebrows. "See?"

Jess laughed lightly. "How can he expect a silent-movie girl out of an all-talking daughter?"

She laughed too. She spotted his shoe boxes in the corner and knelt beside them, glanced back at him as if for sanction, then opened the boxes and began peeling off the pages, scanning his music sheets. "I do talk a lot. But anyway, you get the drift. I'm not doing exactly what he had in mind, but I still want him to be proud of me, and I think he will be."

"I'm not sure it's the same thing, what I was talking about."

"Well, parents are parents. And I think most of them really want their kids to do well and be happy, even if they had something else in mind. They want to be proud of their kids. You disagree?"

"No."

She looked at some more music sheets. "You know, I would have thought he'd be proud that I wanted to follow in his footsteps. He was a top sound engineer. Worked on movies, including some pretty big ones. He let me hang around when I was a little girl, and I fell in love with it. It was like he was working magic. I felt like, Jesus, so much was in his hands. He could make things *sound* good. Boosting or damping, dubbing. That's when I got interested in sound. Show biz in general and movies in particular fascinated me, of course, but I began to develop an ear."

"As a little girl."

"Right. Eventually, I got a job. He didn't even know about it. So while other girls were in the kitchen, I was in the dubbing room—mixing sound instead of stew, you might say. I loved it. I worked hard, and I was good at it."

"Why didn't you stay with it?"

"Well . . ." she chuckled, "he found out about it, of course, because word got around. It made no difference to him whether I was good at it or not, he didn't want me in the business, period. He got me fired."

"Fired!"

"Yup." She chuckled again. "I wouldn't quit, so he got them to fire me. You know the attitude—'No daughter of mine is gonna get into' blah, blah, blah, et cetera, et cetera."

"I know the feeling."

"Yeah, I guess you probably do."

"Did you yell and scream and stomp your foot?"

"No. I was disappointed. But I love him anyway."

"I know that feeling too." Jess nodded. "So how did you get from there to here? From a fired sound engineer to a talent manager?"

She smiled and dug into the second shoe box to look through more music sheets. "Show business was in my blood. Naturally enough, hunh? Once you get a taste. I thought about being an actress, but I didn't want the hassle. Somebody always calling the shots for you, and everything ends up being a variation of the old casting-couch routine. And I wasn't a big, gorgeous beauty, you know. It wasn't very many years ago that there simply weren't roles for women who weren't gorgeous. So anyway, I was nice enough looking but not gorgeous, so it came down to talent, which I didn't have too much of either. I guess that's the bottom line. And you can't guess what I did."

"Became an agent."

"First I tried out for a roller derby team. Don't laugh. I've always been pretty athletic. I swim, of course. I ran track in high school. So I figured, what the hell, the roller derby is show biz, like professional wrestling. Plus it allows you to work off your aggressions and hostilities, which I also had my share of."

"You don't seem hostile to me."

"I'm *not* hostile to you. But what you mean is, well, you're right. I'm not basically a hostile person. The truth is, I wanted to stay in show business, and I like to spot talent and help it get somewhere." Taking a shoe box with her, she went over and sank onto the sofa, pushing her hair back with one hand. "I'll tell you something. Roller derby is the greatest training in the world for what I'm doing now—you get knocked on your ass all the time."

Jess laughed.

"Performers do it to you without the skates."

"How do you mean?"

"Well, you see, I am a manager. It must also be apparent to you that I am not a big-time manager. What you may not see is that I am nonetheless good at it. It's easy for the big agencies, they just take the ones obviously on their way to the big bucks and run with them. You can hardly lose that way. But it's tough where I'm at, looking for talent where nobody else is looking, spotting talent nobody else sees. That means you're taking real chances."

"Because the talent may never get anywhere."

"Well, yes and no. Like I said, I'm good at it, which means that I usually can spot a talent that will get somewhere, given some breaks, a little sleight of hand, some daring maneuvers, et cetera."

"But you said performers knock you on your ass."

"Never fails. Yup, you discover them, help them along, slip them a few bucks for the rent now and then, you know, nurse them along while they sharpen up their act and get it together."

"And?"

"And the minute any of them hits it big, the first thing they do is dump their first manager, the one that got them that far, meaning me. Some big agency always snaps them up, steals them. And I start over, go back to the street looking for some candy store joker with a good voice or a hot piano or a smooth guitar that nobody's ever heard of."

Jess pondered for a moment. "Don't you have a contract with a client?"

"Sure." Molly chuckled. "A hug and a kiss. Easiest thing in the world to tear up."

"But why don't you have written contracts?"

"Oh, I don't know. I guess I just don't think a piece of paper ought to be what ties people together— not even in a marriage. There has to be enough respect and affection." She looked wistful. "And what does my father say when I lose a client? 'Tough luck, hang in there, kid'? Nope. What he says is 'Serves you right, Molly. You shouldn't be in that business in the first place.' Nice, hunh?" She looked at him appealingly. "But it's okay. I understand him, and he doesn't mean any harm. He just doesn't like to see me getting knocked on my ass."

"Natural enough, for a father."

"Like I said, I love him. That's natural too."

"Yeah." Jess turned pensive, wondering about his father, wondering if maybe part of his father's fears

and disappointments in what Jess was trying to do had
its basis in love, in not wanting to see Jess knocked on
his ass. Some of it surely was that, but not all. His
father loved traditions and the synagogue so much too.

"What he doesn't understand," Molly went on,
"and maybe something I don't understand too well
myself, is that I don't really mind when the clients
leave."

"You don't?"

She smiled. "I found them. I discovered them.
Me. And if they turn out to be big, I know it was me
that got them rolling. I have pride, satisfaction. They
can't take *that* away from me."

"No." Jess watched her as she rummaged through
the shoe box. She talked tough sometimes, and clearly
she was tough and plucky. But at the same time she
had such an appealing vulnerability. She was honest.
She was thoughtful and energetic and optimistic. She
was, all in all, a very attractive woman. That recognition caused some guilt to well up in him, and thoughts
of Rivka to flit through his brain. Molly's appreciation
of talent, and her persistence in finding her own path
and helping others find theirs—Jess wished Rivka
thought more that way.

With her books and studies and thesis, perhaps
Rivka was finding her own path. But what troubled
Jess was that she seemed propelled along that path not
so much because it was what she wanted to do, what
she was best at, as because it was what she *ought* to
do. Because of her responsibilities, her obligations, her
guilt for having descended from those who survived the
Holocaust. But it was not *her* holocaust, not really.
Indeed, it was important for people not to forget the
tragedies of that war, the horrific sacrifices and injus-
tices. But to Jess, it was even more important to live,
to accomplish, to find your own way, to use your own
gifts to achieve your own satisfaction and rewards and
pride.

It was this crucial difference of attitude and per-
ception that stood between him and Rivka. It was not
that one of them was necessarily right and the other

wrong. It was just that they were different. "Different-ness," what an unhappy connotation that suggested to him. What an ironic difference in the implications of the word, when applied to just two married human beings instead of unknown thousands or millions.

"What's this one?" Molly's words interrupted his reverie. She held up a set of song sheets. "Seems like it would sound very nice. 'Gentle Game.' Not one of your basic happy-sunshine songs, but nice. Sing a little of it for me?"

"What for?"

"Well, if it's any good, maybe I can place it." She shrugged. "Who knows? While Rabinovitch is cantor-ing, Robin can be collecting royalties."

"I don't think I'm in a selling mood."

"Okay, then just sing it for me. I would like to hear you sing it."

"Just for fun."

"For pleasure. Pleasure's okay, isn't it?"

Jess chuckled. He scratched his head. What the hell, he figured, he couldn't sleep anyway. He went over to his case to take out his guitar and began tuning it.

Molly stooped before the stereo and turned off the Charlie Parker album that had been playing at low volume over and over. What she also did, what Jess didn't see, was to slip a cassette into the tape machine and press the "record" button.

He strummed a bit tentatively. It was a ballad, one he had written some time ago, and he began singing softly, as befitted a small, intimate room:

"Life and loving you is not a gentle game . . ."

In the beginning, Molly stole a few glances at the tape machine to make sure it was picking up properly. But very soon her whole attention was drawn to Jess. She thought she knew his voice by now, but there was a certain quality, a depth and control, that revealed itself particularly in this setting. Even when he sang so softly, there was such strength and dominance. And his phrasing revealed something else; he could sing a song with sad words without pathos, making it move.

". . . Everything I tried to touch with softness . . . has broken into bits too small to see . . ."

She was more captivated than ever before. Not only his voice and phrasing, she realized, was what gripped her. He had himself written these lyrics, himself composed the undulent melody; the music came from deep within him, and described him maybe more than he knew.

He swept into the final verse, seemingly oblivious to her presence, seized by his own music:

"Everything worth having is worth fighting for, and you mean more than anything to me . . . So if I mean the same to you, or something close, please let me know before I set you free . . ."

He struck the final chords, and the room fell suddenly quiet. His eyes were lowered to his guitar, hers were raised to him.

Then she said, "No one should sing your songs but you."

Slowly he looked over at her, almost as if puzzled. Then he blinked and came alive. He quickly put his guitar away, looked at his watch, and said, "I guess we'd better get going."

She didn't answer.

He headed for the bathroom. "I'm just going to splash some water on my face."

He turned on the cold water, cupped his hands to catch it, dipped his face into it. He heard music. He turned off the water and stood still. It was himself he heard, singing the song. It gave him an eerie feeling.

He hurried out. "What's that?"

Molly smiled, leaning back in the sofa, her hands folded behind her head. "I made a demo. A tape. You didn't notice?"

"Why?"

"Well, you won't be here to sing it for people in person, right? So I can listen to it whenever I want. And other people can hear it, maybe."

He listened. He couldn't help being fascinated. It was like being caught by "Candid Camera," except not doing something silly, but doing something you loved to do, what you did best, something proud. He was surprised at the impact it had on him. That was something he preferred not to reveal. So he shrugged and said, "Not bad."

"Not bad at all."

"Well, well, well."

"You didn't think you were a singer?"

"Well, naturally, you know. But I never actually heard myself this way."

"Hmmm." She watched him, hopefully, listening to the music. For a minute he seemed unsure of himself. She let the music work on him. She didn't move.

He stood looking down at the shoe boxes. "I'll leave these here for Bubba. Anything he wants he can have. It's the least I can do."

Molly sprang up, stomped over to the tape player, and switched it off. Angrily she pressed the rewind button and watched the tape spin back. "For Bubba, hunh?"

"Well, and you, if you want."

"Sure. And you can just cut out. Listen, the guy who wrote these songs doesn't want to go back to New York. Maybe *you* do. But not *him,* not the guy who sat down and wrote these words and music for himself to sing." She glared at him. "You came out here for two thousand bucks, you're going home with zilch."

"I'm not complaining."

"Oh, no," she said with biting irony, "you wouldn't complain, not you. Just get knocked on your ass and stay on your ass." She softened her voice. "You could stay. You could give it a shot. You could move in with Bubba. A week, maybe two, something like that. I could get you a job, make some good demos. You could give it that much of a try."

"If I wanted."

"Yeah, if you wanted." She went to the window. The sky was lightening up, it was morning. "I saw what you did to that audience last night," she said almost to herself, looking out at the dawn. "What happened to that audience doesn't happen very often. It was something very special. They knew it was special. And you made a believer out of me." She turned to him. "Jess, I think you could be something, you know? I don't have to say that. There'd be no reason for me to say that unless I really believed it. I think you could be somebody important, maybe more important than you can imagine."

"I don't need to be important."

"You don't know what you need!"

"Is that a fact?"

"Damn right! You are right on the edge of something you thought you wanted a couple of days ago. Why run from it now?"

"I'm not interested, that's why. Don't you understand? I'm just not interested!" He chopped his hand down for emphasis. "I came out here to do a job. I screwed it up. I bombed. That's that!"

"You didn't bomb!" she fired back at him, her hands clenched. "The only bomb you dropped was on Keith Lennox's chin, and he deserved it." She narrowed her eyes and said acidly, "You looked like a fighter, but I guess you're not. You're good for one punch. If that scores, you walk away. But when it comes to really fighting, hanging in for the struggle, then you walk away too. Even when it's something you want. 'Everything worth having is worth fighting for,' hunh? Nice line. When you sang it, I thought you meant it!"

After a pause, he said, "You finished?"

"Yeah."

"So am I. Let's go."

He started for the door. Molly hesitated, then snatched the cassette from the machine and followed him.

Chapter 5

The airport terminal, this early in the morning, was not as crowded and bustling as it had been when he arrived. Jess walked quickly, with long strides. Molly hurried behind him, head down, muttering to herself.

At the departure gate he finally stopped and waited for her. He didn't quite know what to say, what form the goodbye should take.

For an uncomfortable moment she looked at him, a slight smile not expressing warmth. "Is *schmuck* a Jewish word?" she asked calmly.

"Yeah, why?"

She shrugged, the smile faded. "I figured when I saw you off, I just wanted to say something in Jewish to you."

"It's not exactly *'Bon voyage.'* "

"You ain't exactly French, and that isn't exactly what I meant to convey."

Jess laughed and patted her shoulder. "So long, Molly." He turned immediately and went through the gate and down the corridor to the plane.

Molly watched until he was gone from view, then hurried over to a young woman wearing an airline blazer. The woman stood behind a counter over which was a sign: "We're the Airline that always says YES!"

"Excuse me," Molly said, "are you a passenger agent?"

"Yes."

She pointed to the sign. "Is that true?"

"We try," the agent said, smiling. "What can I do for you?"

"Find me somebody with enough authority to do something very special for a very special passenger who just boarded that flight. Unless you have the authority yourself, of course."

"It depends." She still smiled. "What did you have in mind?"

"Well, see . . ." Molly leaned close conspiratorially, "this guy is a big recording star—you'd know his name, but I'd rather not give it, you know how they are. And he's just cut a new song. And today's his birthday. It would be a real treat for him, and a thrill, for the other passengers too, if you could take this cassette . . ."

Jess sat in the filling plane looking moodily out at the vast stretches of concrete and grass. Passengers pushed through, reached up to stuff coats and small bags into the overhead compartments, settled in their seats, some of them alone, some of them jabbering to those accompanying them.

He was not happy to be leaving, not happy to be going home, not happy about anything. But he was doing what he guessed he ought to be doing. Soft, insipid music filled the cabin, meant to be comforting to the passengers. But it was not comforting to him. He couldn't abide music that had no life, no spirit, no point. But you couldn't avoid that music here any more than you could in an elevator. He heaved a deep sigh and closed his eyes.

Then the music cut off. After a minute of quiet, music came on again.

But different. His eyes popped open. Loud and clear, the music was his, was him. It was what he had sung in Molly's living room, what she had recorded. He gripped the armrests. The sweet strains of "Gentle Game" wafted through the plane. He felt his face flush with embarrassment before he realized that nobody would know it was his voice. Passengers began quieting down. He dared to glance around. They were listening!

He was suddenly in turmoil, his stomach tightening. People were smiling, nodding in time to the music!

Molly! What couldn't that broad do? There was nothing *he* could do, in any event, but listen.

The song ended, just as he had ended it then. There was a pause. And then her voice, also just as it had sounded then, came over the sound system:

"No one should sing your songs but you."

Molly looked anxiously out the window at the plane. The cargo carriers were moving away. Soon the jet would be pushed from the terminal.

It had been a big gamble, not because she had so much to lose—nothing, really—but because if it didn't work it would at the very least make it harder for Jess to leave. And she knew it wasn't easy for him anyway. She didn't want to hurt him. The gamble was to risk hurting him in hopes of helping him.

But, glancing at the big airport clock, she guessed she had made a mistake. It wasn't going to work.

The NO SMOKING and FASTEN SEAT BELTS signs flashed on. He couldn't think. There was no time to think. Suddenly he just acted.

He sprang out of his seat, grabbed his guitar case and carryon bag, and dashed for the door. It was just being closed when he slipped through.

He ran down the corridor and was confronted at the end of it by the smiling passenger agent in the airline blazer.

"Happy birthday," she said gaily, holding out the cassette for him.

He froze for a second, staring at the cassette. Then he snatched it and sped on.

Molly was at the gate. Seeing him, she threw up her arms as if signaling for a touchdown, grinning in surprise and relief.

He ran up to her. "Cheap trick . . ." he panted, trying not to smile.

"Okay, come on." She quickly regained her composure. "We've wasted enough time."

"Sneaky . . ."

"So you're not the only one with a sneak punch." She pressed a key into his hand, then slipped her arm through his and started hauling him along. "That's the key to Bubba's pad. You're staying with him. It's all set."

"When did you—"

"Contingency plans, always got them set up. You never know, right?"

"You're . . . something." He was still breathing hard.

"Don't say that, okay? Not yet. We got lots to do, lots of angles to play. We'll stop for a little breakfast—I'll buy, don't worry—then go right to work."

"What work?"

She veered toward the coffee shop. "Well, it won't be driving a cab, bozo. Music work. I gotta warn you, though. Nothing happens overnight. It may take . . ." she smiled up at him, "oh, two or three days."

Jess laughed in spite of himself. "One day with your ideas is like a week of normal life."

"In that case, we can skip breakfast."

"I'm hungry."

"Then be careful what you say."

"I gotta make a phone call. Home."

She slid into a booth, then gave him a leery look. "Be careful what you say there too."

He tried home, got no answer. He called the synagogue, Tillie said Rivka was there, but in the social hall, at a wedding. "Who?" Jess asked quickly.

"Bonnie Jankowitz."

"You mean Bonnie Johnson."

"If you wish."

"Come on, Tillie." Jess always was annoyed with how the synagogue refused to accept people's chosen names. "That's her legal name."

"So, Bonnie Johnson is getting married. The line is busy down there."

"I'll hold." Good for Bonnie, he thought. What a great girl. Deserved the best. He couldn't remember who she was getting.

Finally the phone rang.

"Hello?"

"Rivka! Hello from Hollywood."

"Jess! What happened? Flight delayed?"

"You won't believe what's going on."

"Maybe."

"Well, you know that the album gig didn't work out."

"I'm really sorry about that."

"But the lucky part is, somebody made a demo of me singing."

"What's a demo?"

"Like a quick recording, a tape. You play it for agents, producers, whoever, to get them interested."

"So, you have a nice souvenir to bring home."

"That's just it, Riv. Some people are interested in the demo. So I won't be coming home right away. Riv? Riv?"

"I'm here."

"You're not upset, are you? I mean, this is a really big break."

"So was the album thing."

"No, this is better, really."

"Good for you."

"Riv. Rivka?"

"Who's interested?"

"In the demo? Oh, the names wouldn't mean anything to you. But my manager's handling it."

"Molly."

"Yeah, and—"

"Where will you be staying?"

"With Bubba," he said quickly. "Right with Bubba. Nothing's changed, really. I mean, we were originally planning on two weeks. It won't be more than that."

"Maybe I'll get a pet to keep me company."

"Sure, heh-heh. How's Papa?"

"You want to know how Papa is? Why don't you tell him your news? I'll get him."

"Unh, no, Riv, I've gotta run, an appointment. I'll call you over the weekend, okay?"

"I'm not going anywhere."

They said their quick goodbyes, and Jess hung up. The call didn't make him feel good.

Molly's smiling face over the table in the booth made him feel better. He dug into the scrambled eggs and fried potatoes. "You're not eating?"

"Not hungry."

"So talk to me. Tell me some ideas while I eat."

"Okay. You know Zany Gray?"

"The comedian? Sure."

"He's got a big one-nighter coming up. I just happen to know he just happened to lose his opening act yesterday."

"And?"

"So the spot's made to order for you."

Jess stopped chewing. "How you gonna manage that?"

"Gray's agent is Eddie Gibbs. You remember, from the Morris office? The guy that was at the Cinderella Club?"

"How could I forget? But last I remember, he was saying he hated you."

"True. But he's the key. I'll get to him. There are ways."

"You're something else, you know that?"

"I just like challenges, that's all."

They sat in Molly's car across the street from the William Morris Agency office, where they could see the parking lot.

"He'll be coming out any minute," Molly said.

"How'd you know he had a three o'clock appointment? You said even his secretary hangs up on you."

"Spy in the mailroom. Always pays to keep friends on the lower levels of a big-time operation. They're the ones you can trust."

Jess shook his head. He was highly dubious of this latest plan. But her spirit was infectious, and in fact she seemed able to pull off all sorts of dubious maneuvers—even though nothing had quite worked yet. "The last time you had an idea like this, I got busted."

"So did Eddie Gibbs, don't forget. Which, of course, is a large part of our problem. But I promised I'd have you working in two or three days. This is only the second day."

"Third."

"Sundays don't count. There he is!"

Immediately she pulled on a black slouch hat and dark glasses, and turned up the collar of her jacket to hide her face. She slid out of the car. "Just remember what I told you."

"What's that?"

"Don't *you* do anything!"

She scampered across the street just as Eddie Gibbs strode briskly to his Rolls and got in.

When Eddie started the engine, Molly yanked the passenger door and jumped in.

"Pretend you don't know me," she said in a huskily disguised voice.

Eddie sat bolt upright, facing ahead, as if afraid to look at her. "I don't."

"You will. Shut off the engine. We'll talk."

"You can take my money," he said in a quavering voice. "Just leave me my credit cards."

Molly flipped open her purse and reached into it.

"Okay, okay, you can have the credit cards. Just leave me the picture of my wife and kids, and my—"

"Turn on the tape deck and turn the volume up loud."

He turned it on.

"Close your eyes."

He squeezed them shut so tight that little tears were forced out.

"Now listen and listen good!"

"Anything you have to say, I'll listen. Please just—"

She took the cassette from her purse and jammed it into the tape deck. Suddenly the car was filled with the music of Jess singing "Gentle Game."

Molly let the music pour out for a while. Then she turned the volume down and said, "You like him?"

"Yeah, yeah," he said nervously, "he's good. But what's that got to do with—"

"What do you mean, good? He's terrific!"

"He's terrific," Eddie echoed mechanically. "Who is he?"

"Zany Gray's new opening act!"

"Wait a minute." He opened his eyes. "Who are you?"

Molly pushed her hat back, took off her sunglasses, and smiled at him.

"Molly! Molly Oliver!"

"And that's Jess Robin you're hearing. You heard him at the Cinderella Club."

"What the hell are you trying to do?"

"Solve your problem with Zany Gray."

"You crazy broad!"

"*I* am not the issue, Eddie. Jess Robin is. And you agreed he's terrific."

"I didn't agree to anything! Show me where it says I agreed. You're crazy. *He's* crazy. I don't book nobody from a damned tape! This isn't some fly-by-night agency you're dealing with here! This is William Morris! I don't book anybody I haven't seen in front of an audience!"

"You saw him at the Cinderella Club in New York, like I said."

"Out! Out!" He tilted his face up. "Lord protect me from this babe."

She opened the door and slid slowly out. "Sooner or later you're gonna want him. Or somebody else is."

"He's probably wanted in three or four states already. Out of my way!"

She stepped aside and watched Eddie wheel out of the lot and disappear down Wilshire Boulevard.

She strolled back to her car and flopped heavily into the driver's seat.

"You don't have that opening-act look on your face," Jess said.

"What you get when you try to deal with agents who are deaf, dumb, and blind. Bastard!"

"He didn't like it."

"He loved it."

"But then . . ."

"Some guys you go front door, some guys you go back door. That was front door."

"So now?"

"So now we're going home, to my place, to think."

"And then?"

"I don't know. I just don't know, Jess."

"Uh-oh. You usually do know."

"I usually say I do. We ain't beat, buster. We just lost a round, that's all."

The beach sand felt cold to his bare feet, and the ocean, coal black under the night clouds, looked cold as ice. But the breeze that blew over them was warm. It lifted her hair so that it looked like the graceful wings of a brown gull and made their shirts billow in front of them like spinnakers filling before the wind.

"I feel," Jess said, "like I've been here a hundred years."

"Less than a week. But California does that to you."

"What do you mean?"

"It takes you to its warm bosom."

"Makes you comfortable."

"Yes."

"But I'm not comfortable, Molly."

"Homesick?"

"A little, maybe. Yeah, I guess I am. For New York. For the excitement of New York, for places I know. But I guess mainly I just feel a little useless." He stooped to pick up a small piece of driftwood. "Like a beachcomber." He tossed the wood aside.

"California will do that to you, too."

"I gotta do something, Molly."

"We're working on it."

They walked a while in silence.

"That's what's got me a little puzzled, Molly." He stopped to stare out over the water, his hands jammed in his pockets.

"What?"

"Why are you working on it? I mean, on my case, so much. You're getting nothing out of it."

She stood beside him, her hands shoved into her pockets like his. "I like you, naturally. I wouldn't do it if I didn't. I also think you've got a wonderful talent. I know I'm right."

"Unfortunately, the rest of the music world doesn't share your view."

"Crap. It will. It's all timing. A break here and there. Patience. Persistence. I could never forgive myself for giving up on you, a talent like yours. It would be such a waste."

"You do all this without even a contract—nothing guaranteed at all."

"Well, you know how I feel about contracts."

"You don't believe in them."

She turned to face him. "That isn't what I said."

"Oh, you mean . . ."

"You want a contract, let's draw one up right now. Good a time and place as any."

"Hug and a kiss."

"That's what goes on my dotted line, Jess."

They slowly embraced, then hugged firmly. He kissed her on the cheek.

"I want the whole signature, buster."

She drew herself up to meet his mouth. The kiss too was light at first, then it lingered, grew firm. They moved their mouths together, then Jess pulled away.

"Whew," he said.

"Just business," she said softly.

He held her by the arms and looked at her. "Right."

They resumed walking, now holding hands.

"How's it going at Bubba's?" she asked.

"Crazy. You know how it is. Sleep till noon. Then they all split for work every which way. Sometimes we jam, you know, late at night. Like the old days."

"The old days?"

"When we used to hang out, the bunch of us. We used to get it together in lofts or apartments or even on street corners. Always pulled in some kind of crowd, had a good time. It was always a good time. No pressure. We weren't pretending to be serious musicians or anything, bunch of crazy instruments."

"Like what?"

"Well, Teddy would pull out the old tissue paper and comb. Mel would shake his tambourine. Timmy would use a suitcase or a box when he couldn't find bongos. Bubba would beat his drumsticks on a chair, when he couldn't find a drum. I had a set of maracas. I would sing, they would back me up. Then I started picking up on guitar. And they got instruments too. We started making real music, you know, getting serious about it. The truth is, I kind of miss the old days, when it was just fun."

"It'll be fun again. You need an audience."

He looked at her quizzically. "Why do you say that? That I need an audience?"

"You're a performer, Jess. You have the ego of a performer. Don't look hurt, there's nothing wrong with that. I'm not saying you're a prima donna. But an audience feeds you, lifts you up, makes you feel worthwhile. You get a lot of pleasure out of giving that pleasure to an audience—I've seen it. Otherwise you could sing in the shower."

He laughed. "I do that too."

"I'll have to hear you sometime."

He gave her hand a squeeze. "Business, remember?"

"Right."

Bubba, in baggy pajamas, padded to the bathroom and turned on the water to brush his teeth.

"Bubba, you think anything's ever gonna break?"

"Sher, Jesh."

"What?"

"Jush a sec." Bubba rinsed out his mouth and came into the living room. "I said, sure. That's what show biz is for, right? Hey, my man, don't get down now. Pick your head up. You thinking about your old lady?"

"Sometimes. She hasn't sounded too happy on the phone lately."

"Nothing new about that."

"Hey."

"I just mean, she ain't never been exactly ecstatic about this whole thing, not only about you being out here, but what you're trying to do. I wasn't critizing her. How you feel, that's up to you."

Jess fiddled with his coffee cup and stared idly at the TV, on which was some game show with the sound turned off. "Yeah, how I feel. Sometimes I don't know how I feel. I don't know if I'm doing the right thing."

"Well, nobody knows that but you, my man."

"Some help."

"Hey, listen." Bubba sat down beside him and put a hand on his shoulder. "You know where I'm comin' from, right? And that's that I am your friend. That don't change, no matter what. And as a friend, I don't like to see you hurt no way. But also as a friend, I know that some hurt is just part of movin' on. Dig? Now, what part of your hurt is one thing, what part is the other, that's something I can't know. Ain't nobody can know that but you. Only thing I can do is tell you how *I* feel. And I only do that when you want to know."

"So tell me."

"Well, I see you got yourself a cup of coffee. Why don't you get your friend, Bubba, one while I finish up in the bathroom."

Jess heated up the coffee. When Bubba rejoined him, he sat across the low table facing Jess.

"So?" Jess said.

"I ain't got a lot to say. Mostly I just wanted a cup of coffee." They chuckled together. "First of all, I ain't no marriage counselor. But sometimes you seem like you're swimming upstream with that side of it, so I suppose you got some things to work out, one way or another. All I can say about that is, there ain't nothing that can't be changed, up, down, or sideways. And there ain't nothing that *shouldn't* be changed, when it gives you grief. Okay?"

"Okay."

"So now, on the business side. No question about your talent. I mean, all we got to do is get people to hear you. Why that ain't happened yet, who knows?

Molly's working. We all been passing the word. What you got to face, my man, is that it may not work. Not ever. That's reality."

"So what you're saying is that to face reality, I ought to pack my—"

Bubba held up his hand. "I ain't saying pack nothin'. Reality is that it may not work, but it is also that it may work. That's the risk. Now, my view of this particular reality is that we keep knocking at the door, the door's gonna open for you. You're that good. Sooner or later, that door's gonna open. All we need is time."

"Two weeks, it's been. Seems like a lifetime."

"Two weeks ain't shit, my man. Think about what you're saying. Two weeks. But see, your two weeks ain't nobody's two weeks but yours, how much time that is and whether you can afford it. Maybe that's all the time you got. That's up to you. I can't say two weeks is not enough for you, all I can say is two weeks ain't diddly to wait for a music gig to open up in L.A. for a Jewish boy from New York who ain't never had no real gig of his own in his life."

Jess nodded. He studied Bubba, but Bubba avoided his eyes. "Okay, Bubba, give it to me straight. Tell me what you think I should do, how you feel."

"Hang in. Just as long as you can, hang in. And when you can't hang in no longer, split. Then you done all you can."

Jess sighed. "Rivka wants me back, Papa wants me back, I'm supposed to be a cantor . . ."

"You gonna be here tonight?"

"Well, I'm going over to Molly's later, chat with her awhile. Then I think maybe I'll fly home."

"Tonight."

"Yeah."

Bubba scratched his stubbly chin. "Well, that don't give me much time. But at least that gives me today. One more shot. I'll call you by seven o'clock. Wait for my call, okay?"

"You got it."

Bubba smiled and thumped his fist down lightly on Jess's hand.

Molly was at the piano, picking out the melody line from Jess's "Love on the Rocks" with one finger.

Jess was on the phone. "You sure? . . . Yeah, okay . . . Well, tell him to call me at Molly's as soon as he gets in."

He hung up and turned to Molly. "Bubba's not there. He said he'd call at seven and it's almost quarter to eight."

"Like you need a fix or something."

"He said seven."

"Jesus, since when do people in this business go by the clock, except to tell one day from another?"

"It's just driving me nuts, that's all."

"I think you should just cool it. I think, in fact, that Bubba will come through with a last-minute gig."

"Out of the blue."

"Not so out of the blue. I have a lot of confidence in Bubba, given the situation."

"Why?"

"He's got a lot of pull at the Venice Blues."

"He's a *waiter!* What kind of pull you got as a waiter?"

"Bubba's not your everyday waiter."

"He's *been* there every day, and hasn't turned up anything."

"Today's a brand-new day. Hey, just relax. Have faith, *cantor*. Believe! Make your mind a positive force."

"My mind feels like a pinball machine."

She shuffled some music sheets around on the piano and began picking out another melody with her finger. "Hey, this is pretty. No title. What do you call it?"

" 'Hello Again.' " He sat down next to her and filled in some notes.

"Strange title."

"Yeah, kind of weird, I guess. But it was kind of weird how it happened. I wrote it about a phone call, a wrong number."

"A song about a wrong number?"

"Yeah." He leaned over the keyboard thoughtfully. "I was about eighteen, nineteen. I was calling a friend, a guy I hung out with. I dialed the number and this girl answered. She said I had the wrong number, but she was so nice about it, friendly—you know, not the 'Wrong number,' click! So we talked for a little while, just friendly. And that was that. A few days later, I got the same wrong number, her again. And we talked again. We seemed to have a lot to talk about. It was very nice, very comfortable. So after that, I started calling her on purpose. She became a fantasy girl, a kind of dream girl to me. So obviously the next step was—"

"You met her, and she didn't stand up to your fantasy."

"I never met her." Jess plunked some notes idly. "We made a date once, but I didn't go. I was scared, I guess. A few days after that, I worked up the courage to call her again, and she said she hadn't shown up for our date either. We were both afraid of spoiling it."

"Gee, that's too bad."

Jess shrugged. "Maybe not. We'll never know. She moved away, and I pictured myself years later dialing a wrong number again. And she'd answer the phone. That's how I'd find her. I had that fantasy for a long time."

"I wonder if she had the same thoughts."

"Well, that was part of my fantasy, that she was waiting, somewhere, for me to call."

"So then you wrote the song, about your dream of finding her again."

"Sort of." He began to play and sing. "Hello again, hello ... Just called to say hello ... I couldn't sleep at all tonight ... And I know it's late ... But I couldn't wait ..."

After a few bars, he stopped. "That's as far as I got."

"Why?"

"I don't know. I couldn't figure out how the conversation would have gone. I started thinking about it too practically, too realistically. I stayed as unfinished as the fantasy."

"It's beautiful. You have to finish it."

"Some day. Maybe. Back in New York, maybe.

Maybe tomorrow I'll just sit in my apartment and
bring back the dream. That's the reality of it."

"Bubba's going to call. You'll have a reality right
here."

"Nope." He looked at his watch. "It's getting too
late."

Molly paced around the room while he noodled
aimlessly at the piano. She snapped her fingers. "I
know how to get you to stay. I'll give you my body.
That will keep you in California for a while, anyway."

He looked up a moment, then resumed picking
out chords.

"Hey! I just offered you my body!"

"I heard."

"What is it with you? You rather have a pizza?"

He chuckled and turned around on the bench,
crossed his legs and folded his hands over his knee.
"Listen, Molly, these last two weeks have been terrific
for me, really. I saw so much I thought I'd never see.
And you've been more than terrific. You're amazing.
You're fun. You taught me a lot. I hope I can repay
you somehow, someday."

"Super. So much for all our work, all my hopes.
So much for my goddamn body!"

Jess laughed, and she joined him in it. He turned
back to the piano.

The phone rang and she jumped for it. "Bubba?
... Bubba! ... What? ... Yes! ... Great! ... *Wow!*
... I'll ask the local cantor." She held the phone away
from her mouth. "Jess, will you still be here at ten
thirty tonight?"

"I can be, why ..." Jess was already on his
feet.

"To play a gig at the Venice Blues Club."

"But ... how ... yes! Are you crazy? Yes!"

"Okay, Bubba, the cantor can make it ... Eddie
Gibbs? Of course, I already thought of that. He'll be
there, guaranteed. See you there."

Before she even had a chance to hang up, Jess

grabbed her in a hug, swung her off the floor, and spun her around.

The Venice Blues Club was a popular, energetic hot spot sandwiched between other low buildings housing daytime businesses. The fervid atmosphere of its bustling, spotlighted interior radiated to the sidewalk and street where the eclectic clientele gathered—couples in suits, ties, long dresses; punk followers with pins in their ears; leisure-clad singles in dark glasses; even people on disco roller skates. Inside, the tables were arranged close together, and each had a candle in a deep red glass globe.

It was a packed house, but Jess had no time to be intimidated. Bubba met them at the door and hustled Jess backstage. Jess tuned his guitar nervously while Bubba went to the stage mike and held up his hands for quiet.

Bubba wasted no time. He laid out a straight, quick introduction:

"Okay, everybody—giving you a hot new talent from New York—Jess Robin!"

Jess had not worked out a program, he didn't even know how many songs he was supposed to sing. All he knew, when he walked onto the stage and heard the applause, was that he would open with something that moved: "You, Baby."

He adjusted the mike, found Molly at a ringside table, and knew that the empty chair beside her meant that Eddie Gibbs had not shown up.

Hell with it, he was on.

He hit the opening chords. "Hey!" he barked as he launched the driving rhythm. "Hey! . . . Hey! . . . Hey! . . ." Having pumped it up, he finished the chord progression and took it from the top:

"Hey, it takes a lot of time if you want it right . . . Takes a lot of time and it takes believin' . . . You gotta see the signs and you'll get it right . . ."

He had gauged it right; the audience was eager and he had come on hard and fast. He felt the heads bobbing, the shoulders swaying, the fingers snapping.

"Hey! . . . Hey! . . . Take a look, my feet are dancin',
my heart is ready for romancin' . . .

And he wrapped it up leaning on it hard: ". . .
You, baby, baby! Baby, it's *you!*"

He bowed to the applause and cheers, but the
chair next to Molly was still empty. He didn't dare
hesitate and let that empty chair get to him. He swung
immediately into the slower but still upbeat "Dazed
and Confused."

"What's the hurry? Why is eveybody rushing
through? . . . All of it is over, soon enough . . . We go
by just this once . . . Let's not do it so dazed and so
confused . . ."

In the middle of the song, Eddie Gibbs came in,
looked around, saw Molly, and joined her at the table.
The sight lifted Jess like a wave, he felt his voice
loosen, felt the edge of power that came always when
the time was right; the gig was a big break, now it was
complete. He could really let it out for Eddie Gibbs.

He finished, let the ovation wash over him,
stepped back from the mike and nodded over the
vibrant audience. When the noise died down, he
stepped back to the mike already strumming the opening strains of a soft ballad, "Songs of Life." He had
drained off some of the crowd's energy, captured them,
and now he serenaded them:

"Songs of life, they ring . . . From quiet steeples
to distant valleys . . . Along the hillsides . . . Of lovers'
hearts . . . Of lovers' hearts . . . Come sing your songs
of life . . . And they will keep you . . . From ever wanting . . . From ever needing . . . Forever more . . . Forever more . . ."

Just before the end of that, Eddie Gibbs rose and
left as quickly as he'd come. Jess struggled to maintain
his voice, to keep the warmth even when he felt the
little chill of failure as he watched Gibbs go.

Fortunately the song was, as he sang, "not long."
The audience were on their feet begging for more. But
Molly left quickly. Jess fled the stage, out the side
door, and dashed for the front.

He came barreling around the corner of the building just in time to see Gibbs's green Cadillac roll away, and Molly standing on the curb watching it.

He slid to a stop just behind her. "I blew it. He hated me."

Molly turned slowly to him, not smiling but not frowning either. "No. Me, he hates." She started to smile.

"Don't give me that, Molly. That's it. No more. No more show-biz optimism, hopes, ideas, plans, back doors. No more shit. Don't even smile. I'm all—"

"Save it, buster. I dragged Gibbs here on his anniversary. He had to get back to his wife. But you, *you* he loves!"

"What?"

"I been trying to tell you for weeks! Guy like that, he doesn't have to be hit over the head. He doesn't have to listen to you for hours. He just had to hear you and see you. He heard and saw, Jess! You open with Zany Gray next week!"

"But he . . . but I . . ."

"We got a contract?"

Jess grabbed her in a bear hug, kissed her, and let out a rebel yell.

She pulled away suddenly. "Hey you like mushrooms and anchovies?"

"Hunh?"

"Come on." She took his arm, "the best pizza place in town's right around the corner. It may not be my body, but at least I'm buying."

Chapter 6

They had no sooner sat down than Bubba and the brothers strode through the doors of the Pizza Palace.

"Whooee!" cried Teddy from across the room.

"A star is born!" Mel yelled.

Such a disturbance might have bothered the stunned patrons ordinarily, but the four faces were so joyful, the movement through the small restaurant so quick, that neither drunkenness nor hostility was suggested. The patrons simply stopped in mid-slice to watch.

The brothers gathered around Jess, clapping his back, slapping his palms, mussing his hair.

"What you got here," Bubba announced to the gazing patrons, "is a singer named Jess Robin! And before you all reach your next birthdays, he's gonna be a household word and you all gonna be buying his records like the old folks bought Sinatra!"

People muttered approval, whispered to each other, craned their necks to get a look, waved their pizza slices.

"Embarrassed?" Molly asked, leaning across the table.

"He better not ask me to sing."

"Bubba's got taste, bozo."

"So now . . ." Bubba hauled up a chair, the others did the same, crowding around the table. "How's it feel, Mr. Jess Robin sir?"

98

"Good, Bubba, real good."

"You almost lost the faith, child."

"Yeah."

"But you hung in."

"I was about to leave when you called."

"But you didn't. And now you can't. And not just 'cause you got a gig, but 'cause we *all* got a gig. We'll be backing you up. You got *responsibilities* now, my man."

The waiter approached the table cautiously. "Would you like . . . to order?"

Bubba threw a big arm around the man's waist and drew him in. "Don't you be nervous now, friend, just because you're in the presence of a big new star. You gonna be part of the party. Yes sir, I believe we'll have a little bit of everything and a whole lot of beer."

Jess backed his chair out. "Gotta make a phone call."

"Spread the good news, my man."

Jess went to the pay phone in the rear and pulled the glass door shut. He dialed. It rang four times before Rivka answered. "Me, Riv. I know it's late. Sorry to wake you up. But I've got great news."

"You didn't wake me up. I've been working on my thesis."

"Three o'clock in the morning?"

"I felt like it. Also, Harris was lonely, his first night here."

"Harris?"

"I bought a pet, Jess. An Airedale."

"What the hell's an Airedale?"

"A dog. A nice terrier. What's the great news? You coming home?"

"Well, um, sure, but not tomorrow. I got a gig—"

"Not tomorrow."

"Listen, Riv, 'cause this is a terrific break, what we've been waiting for. I'm opening with Zany Gray. You know, the big comedian?"

"I've seen him on TV."

"Yeah. It's only one night. I'm his new opening act."

"One night."

"Yeah. Next week. But it could lead to much more."

"I see."

"Yeah. So, unh, that's the news. How you doing? So you got a dog? How'd that happen?"

"I wanted some company. A couple on the upper West Side—she's on TV here, and he's a writer—very busy people. They just couldn't handle Harris anymore, because he needs a lot of attention. And I have plenty of time to give him attention. I'm always here."

"What kind of name is Harris for a dog?"

"He's beautiful. So playful and loving, like a person. They named him Harris."

"Unh-hunh. So listen, Riv. This is so exciting out here."

"I can imagine."

He hesitated a moment, then said impulsively, "Riv, come out to L.A. and see the show!"

"How could I?"

"I can afford to—"

"I'm rushing to turn in my thesis."

"Come on, another week wouldn't make a difference."

"It's already been two weeks, Jess, and it's already made a difference."

"What are you talking about?"

"Oh, I don't know. I've been thinking. About us."

"Me too. We have a lot to talk about. That's why you should come—"

"Jess, what are you doing? What's going on?"

"What am I doing! This is everything we've been working for!"

"We?"

"Yeah. We're all sitting around this pizza place, Bubba and the guys, celebrating, you know, and Molly."

"Molly."

"Yeah, she's been knocking herself out. She's made it all possible."

"I can't wait to thank her."

Jess saw Bubba beckoning, the pizzas had arrived. "Look, Riv, this is something I gotta do. Think about coming out, okay? And tell Papa—"

"You'll have to tell Papa yourself. I won't cover for you anymore."

"I wasn't going to ask you to. Is he up?"

"He is now. Hold on."

He heard some muffled conversation on the other end of the line Bubba beckoned again.

"Yussel?"

"Hi, Papa. How are you? You all right?"

"Yes, yes. What's this you're staying longer?"

"Riv'll tell you all about it. It's a wonderful opportunity. One more week. Two at the most."

"And if something else happens?"

"Well, who knows? I'm guaranteed one night's show, that's all. We'll worry about something else if it happens when it happens."

"The Jankowitz girl got married. She wished you were here for it."

"Bonnie Johnson, I know. Give her my best."

"And the Siegel boy. His parents won't bar mitzvah him until you come back. That's what they think of you. And Yussel, the rabbi was talking to me just today. He said he's been thinking about your idea, and maybe it would be good to have the English translation of the Sh'ma."

"That's great, Papa. Just great."

"So a lot of people are thinking of you . . ."

"Now listen to me, Papa." He felt suddenly sad for the old man whose loneliness for his son was clear in his voice, but whose pride kept him from pleading for his return. "It's all gonna work out, Papa. I promise you. You'll be proud of me."

Bubba was walking toward the booth.

"A husband's place is with his wife, Yussel," his father said with sudden firmness, "if you want an old man proud."

"I know. I'll be there. I can't wait to see you. I gotta run. Now you take care of yourself and don't worry. I'll keep in touch. Give my love to everybody. G'bye, Papa."

He hung up just as Bubba pulled the booth door open.

"I figured you were talking so long you just might be talking yourself into trouble," Bubba said. "And you gonna miss your own party out here."

Jess wiped a tear away. "No trouble. People just don't understand."

"We do. Or at least *I* do. But trying to explain it to folks now ain't gonna work. They'll understand after you get it *done*. How's your old lady?"

"Typing away. I need a beer."

"Pitcherful do you?"

"Maybe two."

"Then come on. We got 'em."

It was dusk, and the tan stucco of the huge auditorium took on desert hues.

At the top of the broad marquee were the words: ONE NIGHT ONLY. Just below it in much larger letters was: ZANY GRAY! ! ! Beneath that in smaller letters and numbers were the admission prices for the various seat locations. Men working from a cherry-picker lift hoisted from the bed of a truck were just putting up the last and lowest and smallest letters: ALSO: JESS ROBIN.

Cars were pouring into the lot and lining up at the main entrance to let people out. Fans were crowding toward the gates. It was a carnival atmosphere, people carrying flags and banners—ZANY'S FLAKES; ZANY WE LOVE YOU! One man in a Dracula cape and made-up face held a sign reading ZANY'S ZOMBIE.

Around at the side, a cab pulled up at the stage-door entrance, and Rivka got out, carrying a small traveling bag with an airline tag on it.

The auditorium was already near capacity, and the pit band was playing popular tunes.

The sound carried into the small, cluttered dressing room where Jess and the brothers were checking their instruments.

"How you feeling?" Bubba asked.

Jess gave him a wan smile. "Don't let my years in show business fool you—I'm scared."

"You? No way!" Bubba scoffed. "You'll be a smash."

"Sure a long way from the Lower East Side."

"Don't you believe it, my man. Hey, remember how we used to jive on the street corner? The way people would start gatherin' around? They'd listen and smile and clap and tell us how great we were?"

"Yeah, so?"

Bubba waved toward the door. "They're the same people out there tonight. Oh, sure, maybe they're wearing a better class of threads, and maybe they got a little more bread in their pockets. But it's the same people. And you know the best part?"

"What?"

"We don't have to jump outta the way of cars!"

They laughed and skinned palms.

There was a fast knock on the door, and Molly's voice. "Jess, Bubba! Let's go! Show time!"

They filed out.

Molly took his arm. "You okay?"

"Yeah."

"They're gonna love you!"

"Just so I don't have to fight my way out."

They stood in the wings while the lights came down in the auditorium and the spotlights focused on the announcer.

"Ladies and gentlemen, Zany Gray proudly presents a fine, new young singing talent—Jess Robin!"

Jess came out, followed by Bubba and the brothers, and the spotlights crisscrossed to pick them up. They were greeted with polite applause and the general hubbub of an audience waiting for their favorite comedian.

Jess nodded at the audience, scanned it for a few moments, then turned his back on it to face the brothers. "They're not ready for music, Bubba. So we gotta bring 'em around in a hurry. We're changing the program. Open up with 'Summer Love.'"

"You sure, man?"

"Hit it!"

The Brothers Four cranked up some good country-and-western rhythm, Jess caught the beat with his guitar, and turned dramatically back to the mike to open in uncharacteristic style, a quick-paced number he had written years before as a joke, almost a talking song:

"Don't bother me about where I been; I'm all wore out by the shape I'm in . . . Ain't got no stomach for none o' your chin; too much o' your lip's gettin' under my skin . . ."

It was a good, brisk beat for the audience, and he picked it up:

"Don't shake your fryin' pan in my face; cookin' won't get you anyplace . . . 'Cause I been out with the human race; and I didn't get full, but I got me a taste . . ."

He let the brothers carry the rhythm for a few bars, feeling the audience turn more and more to the stage, quieting down, beginning to ride with the tempo.

"Don't give me none of that lonely stuff; 'cause just right now I ain't lonely enough . . . You ain't dealin' with no powder puff; if you don't smooth it down, I'll make it rough . . ."

Molly, in the wings, surprised at the song, was enjoying it, tapping her foot. Behind her, a girl approached the guard, asked him something, and was directed over to Molly.

She tapped Molly on the shoulder. "I'm Rivka Rabinovitch."

Molly gaped at her.

"Robin."

Molly blinked hard and put a hand to her chest. "Oh. Hi."

"Hello."

"Jess'll be surprised."

"I'm a little surprised myself. It was all spur of the moment."

"Unh, I'm Molly. Oliver."

"I know. The guard told me."

They directed their attention back to the stage.

Jess went on: "... And I don't feel like I done you dirt; the pain ain't bad 'cause I don't hurt ..."

Eddie Gibbs came up, trailed by Zany Gray. They ignored the two women.

"You got a great opening act, Zany," Eddie said.

"I didn't know I needed one. He some kind of country boy?"

"Naw, naw, he's just, well, wait'll you hear him really sing."

Jess wound it up: "... Let's have us a beer and go turn in; tomorrow morning we'll start again."

The audience whooped it up.

Rivka eyed Molly. "Jess says you've been a great help to him. Every time we talk, it's Molly did this, Molly did that."

"That's very nice of him."

The lights changed, came in tighter on Jess, and the band segued into the introduction for the soft ballad "My Louise."

They listened to him sing the first verse of the lyrical melody.

"He's good," Rivka said, "no?"

"He's better than good," Molly said. "He's sensational."

Rivka pondered that, listening to Jess. "You have to forgive me," she whispered, choosing her words carefully, "but three thousand miles away, you begin to wonder if he's telling me, well, everything."

Molly smiled and touched her arm. "I once offered him my body, but he settled for pizza."

Rivka laughed pleasantly, and gestured a shy apology. She watched Jess finish the song and step back to lower his head in recognition of the cheers that rose up. Eddie Gibbs clapped loudly, holding his hands high in front of him. Even Zany Gray added some light claps.

"Well, Rivka," Molly said, "I guess the father sent the daughter-in-law to bring the son home, right?"

"You don't understand, Molly. I don't think you *can* understand. There is so much history and tradition, going back so many hundreds of years, and then

Hitler, and our parents, so many things to hold on to . . ."

On the stage, Jess nodded at the band, and they began "Gentle Game."

". . . So you see," Rivka went on, lowering her voice again, "what he comes from, what is part of him, deep down, his differentness, *our* differentness, is something I don't think others can understand."

Molly leaned close to her ear to whisper. "You're right, I don't understand where he comes from. I know very little about his past, about you, or about the hold you and all the traditions have on him. But I sure know where he's going." She motioned to the stage. "Listen to him. Look at him."

They could see the effect Jess was having on the rapt audience.

When he finished and bowed his head, the applause was louder than before. People stood. A few bravos were heard. Jess raised his head to nod around at the crowd, smiling, his face proudly calm.

"I'll tell you one thing," Molly said, raising her voice above the din, "I'm not your problem, Rivka, not by a long shot." She extended both her arms, one toward Jess, the other sweeping the auditorium. "That's your problem. That's a real love affair!"

There were cries of "More!" and "Encore!" But Jess begged off, waving to the audience as he backed away, presenting the brothers who also bowed. Then they quickly left the stage as the announcer entered from the opposite side.

"And now," came the announcer's amplified voice, "the star of our show—Zany Gray!"

Zany swept by them onto the stage. Jess pushed off to the wings, meeting first a welcoming committee of stagehands and others who reached for him to shake his hand and pat him on the back.

"Where's Molly?" Jess called, trying to see over the heads. Finally breaking free, he came face to face with Rivka. He stared at her, stunned.

"Molly thought we ought to be alone for a while," Rivka said softly, an ironic edge to her voice.

"Rivvie . . . when . . . I mean, why didn't you let me know? You heard me sing? When did you—"

"Shouldn't we say hello first?"

Jess recovered enough to embrace her. Several stagehands and members of the technical crew continued to slap him on the back and offer congratulations.

Zany had begun his routine, and the stage manager whispered, "Keep it down!"

"Come on," Jess took Rivka's arm, "we'll go to my dressing room."

Once they were in the corridor, away from the stage, Jess said, "Wasn't that something? That audience? Wow! It's like a thrill I can't explain. I'm so glad you were here."

She raised her eyebrows dubiously, but he wasn't looking at her. "You were wonderful, Jess. The crowd loved every minute, loved you."

"Whew! That's really hard work. Such a big place, you know? All the noise at the beginning. I took a chance with my opener, but I think it worked."

"Everything seemed to work just fine."

"Yeah. And Eddie Gibbs, a really big agent, he was there. Molly introduce you? Wow, it was something."

"It was something, all right."

"I know it's only one night, but I think I'm really on my way. If only Papa could have been here too."

"Tonight you didn't need Papa. You didn't need anybody."

"Hey, of course I did. Bubba and the guys. Molly. And it meant an awful lot that you were there."

"You didn't know I was there."

"But *now,* coming off the stage and finding you, knowing you heard, that means something. A lot."

"Does it?"

"You know what it means for us?"

"Everything you've ever wanted."

"Everything *we* ever wanted."

"Well, what I wanted . . ."

They reached the dressing room, and Jess swung

the door open to find a small party in progress. Bubba
and the brothers, some other musicians and their girl-
friends, and even Eddie Gibbs.

Before Jess could say anything, Eddie came bustling over, bringing another man with him, a spiffily
dressed young guy with curly hair and big rings on his
fingers.

"Jess!" Eddie reached for him. "Hey, come in,
kid. There's someone I want you to meet."

"Unh," Jess backed off, "in a couple minutes,
Eddie."

He closed the door and turned back to Rivka.
"Something's bothering you."

"I don't belong here, Jess. I belong home. That's
where I want to be, with you."

"Sure, but I can't come right now. I mean, things
are breaking, a whole lot of things that could—"

"I understand." She hesitated and looked down at
her feet. "You can't do both."

"Well, just not at the same time."

"So I guess you have a choice to make." She
raised her sad eyes to him.

"A choice?"

She nodded.

"Hey, Riv, how can I go back to the shul, I mean,
right away? After tonight? No way."

"I'm not asking you to. I wouldn't ask."

"Then what are you saying?"

"What I'm saying, I guess, is that I always liked
being married to a cantor."

"Riv, did you ever think that there may be another kind of life that's more exciting, more—"

"Like what? Following a husband around from
city to city saying 'Wow'?"

A pretty blonde in tight silk pants and spike heels
brushed by, gave Jess the eye, and headed into the
party.

Jess kept his eyes on Rivka. "I don't believe it,
Riv. The most important night of my life, and you
want me to come back to—"

"The most important?"

"One of the most important."

"Jess, it's where we come from and what we are. Maybe you can break away from it, but I can't."

"God," Jess looked away and shook his head, "I should have moved you out of that apartment years ago. You're sounding more and more like Papa."

"That's so bad? To sound like your father?"

"I didn't mean it that—"

"Anyway, I've always been like him, Jess. You're the one who's changed."

Two musicians passed in the corridor, calling compliments: "Great job, Robin . . . Terrific gig."

Jess nodded his thanks. He stepped closer to Rivka and took her face in his hands, spreading his fingers over her cheeks. "Riv, we've known each other half our lives. We've been through so many things together, good times, a lot of tough times."

"Yes."

"We know each other so well."

"Maybe not anymore." Her voice firmed. "Anyway, that's what I think, you have a choice only you can make."

"Wait a minute." He studied her. "Are you telling me that unless I come home now it's all over?"

"Well, a choice. I've made mine."

"But that's what you're telling me?"

She thought for a moment, meeting his eyes. "I would like you home only if you come home without any regrets."

The door opened abruptly, Eddie leaned out and grabbed Jess. "Okay, you two, time's up for private chat. People waiting for you, Jess. Now it's time to meet Barney Callahan. He's from Capitol, wants to talk about a record deal."

He dragged Jess into the dressing room. "Hey, Barney! I finally got him. Here he is, the sweetest Robin this side of Delancey Street!"

The curly-haired man took Jess's hand in both of his own and shook it vigorously.

Jess tried to turn back to the doorway, but was held in Callahan's grip. He had only enough of a glimpse to see that Rivka was gone.

Molly opened the door to find Jess standing in the pouring rain, water dripping off the bill of his Greek fisherman's cap. His hands were jammed into the pockets of his windbreaker, which was soaked through and hung on him like the skin of a dead chicken. He stood as if he'd grown from the spot, emotionless as a tree trunk.

"You didn't come to the party," he said dully.

"Jess! Come in, come in." She waved him through the door. "Let me get some of those wet things off you."

"I'm okay."

"Well, my *floor's* not." She snatched off his hat and unzipped his jacket. "Take your shoes off too."

"Why didn't you come to the party after the gig?"

"I figured you could use the time with your wife."

"She went back to New York, right afterward. We talked for a few minutes, then she took off." He handed her his jacket, then knelt to remove his sodden shoes.

"Oh? Just like that?"

"Just like that."

"Well, um . . ."

"And where've you been? I called."

"Here and there, busy. I've got other things in my life besides the career of Jess Robin, you know." She smiled.

"Of course I know that. I just wondered. There was this guy at the party, Callahan, his name was, he wanted me to—"

"I know all about that. It's terrific. Gimme your shoes, I'll dry them." She stuffed some newspaper into the shoes and put them near the radiator and turned up the heat.

"But it was all Eddie Gibbs, you know? He was telling me this, telling me that, I should do this, that. People were partying. I got confused. You should've been there."

"That great, hunh?"

"No, I mean, to help me figure out what the hell was happening. To tell me what to do."

"Eddie Gibbs is tops in that business, don't worry about it."

"Aren't you my manager? Haven't we got a contract?"

"Sure." She smiled slyly and cocked her head. "You want to renew it?"

"But doesn't that mean you should be handling everything?"

"Go sit down. I'll get you a drink. Scotch okay? Jesus, how'd you get here in this rain? I could've picked you up." She went into the kitchen. "Go ahead and talk. I can hear you."

"Well, what am I supposed to do?"

"About what? Your wife? Your album? Your clothes?"

"My *career*. What about my music and stuff, performing?"

She came in carrying two drinks and put them down on the coffee table and sat down next to him. "The album deal is in the best possible hands, like I told you. I don't need to be involved. What, you want another gig? I can book you into the Venice Blues any time you want. And with a little work and time, I can probably get you bigger stuff now. That what you want?"

He picked up his drink and turned the glass in his hands. "I don't know."

"Ah."

"What's that supposed to mean?"

"It isn't your *career* that's bothering you."

"Well, I suppose not—well, it *is,* actually, in a way. I don't know what to do, whether to junk it or not. Rivka wants me to come back. I guess a lot of people are depending on me. Rivka, Papa, the synagogue—it's all part of the same thing. I can't take care of all that and have a career too."

"You lump in a marriage with all the rest. Isn't a marriage kind of a separate matter?"

"Not in this case. Rivka really wants to be part of all that, her whole life is wrapped up in it. She wants mine to be too."

"So, my boy," she patted him on the head, "what can Aunt Molly do to help you?"

"You could start by not making a joke out of everything."

"Sorry. I shouldn't, I know. I know it's a serious thing."

"We been together a long time. We had so many hopes."

"You talk to Bubba about it?"

"Yeah. He says that kind of thing is up to me, he's not a marriage counselor."

"Neither am I."

"I don't want you to be." Jess felt a little defensive. "You know, it strikes me, I really don't know much about you at all. You probably know more about me."

"Maybe." She stretched casually. "Not much to know."

"What do you do—I mean, you know, when you're not working?"

She chuckled. "I either stay home alone or go out alone, or stay home with company or go out with company. I cook when I feel like it, go to movies when I feel like it, swim, run on the beach, read a book, surf, watch TV, go roller skating, sail, dance . . ."

"With somebody."

"You like to dance alone?"

Jess forced a chuckle.

"Any other questions about my life?"

"No, I guess not."

"Well, then, I guess you'll have to excuse me." She looked at her watch. "I have to get ready to go out."

"Oh, sorry." He drained his drink and got up.

"Nothing to be sorry about. I'm afraid your clothes aren't very dry. I'll drop you off someplace, wherever you want."

"No thanks, I'd rather walk. I like to walk in the rain."

"Suit yourself." She got his shoes and jacket. "Soggy, the whole bunch."

He wiggled his feet into his shoes.

"Ever write a song about it?"

"Wet clothes?"

"Walking in the rain."

"Everybody's written songs about walking in the rain."

"Not your way." She accompanied him to the door and opened it. "Rain's let up. Funny about you wanting to know about my life."

"Why?"

"I do normal, everyday things, you do normal everyday things. The major difference between us is that you're married and I'm not."

Jess stepped through the door as he pulled on his black cap and turned up his jacket collar. "Big difference."

"Yup. In some ways it's big. In other ways it's just incidental."

"I don't quite follow."

"I think it's a question of how much you worry about it, one way or the other. I'm not worried about not being married." She laughed. "Hey, listen, come by again, okay? Whenever you feel like it. I like to see you."

"You do?"

"I'll let you know if I don't. Keep in touch, anyway. That album thing is gonna get you to take off. So keep in touch."

"Then answer your damn phone."

"I do, when I'm home." She smiled.

"That ain't often, Molly." He smiled back.

"In that way we're pretty much alike."

"How's that?"

"Neither one of us is all that hot on staying home. Later."

"Later."

He walked off into the drizzle, not knowing if he felt better or worse.

"Hey, Bubba, you rhinoceros!"

"You ain't exactly Miss Twinkletoes neither, hot dog."

Jess held onto the rail. Bubba glided over to him, his roller skates veering this way and that as if they had a mind of their own. Just as he reached for the rail, his legs splayed, and he flopped hard on his rear.

"Oooh, that floor's a mother!" Bubba rubbed his behind, rolled over to plant his hands on the floor, and eased his way erect, but facing the wrong way from the rail. He started gliding back toward the middle of the rink.

"Where you going?"

"I figure . . . Jess . . ." he waved his arms for balance, "that it's easier . . . to just go . . . in the direction I'm headed . . . rather than try and turn . . . 'cause this way I'll eventually find the goddamn rail someplace!"

Jess skated cautiously after him, hoping other skaters could avoid him because he certainly couldn't avoid them.

They met at the other side, where both of them got firm grips on the wooden railing.

"Whooo!" Bubba exhaled. "Why you got me doin' this anyway? Why we gotta be skaters all of a sudden?"

"It's the rage."

"Haw! You want rage, I'll take you back to the Cinderella Club and find that big dude that was after your ass. That fight was easier'n this."

"You said your old lady skated."

"She did. She also ain't my old lady anymore."

"You looking for another one?"

"Nope."

"Why not?"

"Rather just hang out. Look out!"

A careening couple, hands locked together but legs out of control, bounced off the rail, spun around, and tumbled into Jess, knocking him sliding away on his backside.

"Sorry! Sorry!" the man wailed. "You okay?"

"He's fine," Bubba said, controlling his laughter. "Worst thing is, it took him so long to get here. Now I'm gonna have to wait another fifteen minutes for him to crawl on back."

The couple started to help Jess up, but he waved them off, realizing that they'd just end up toppling onto him. He managed to roll back to Bubba.

"Hey, my man, tell me the truth, why we doing this?"

"I just want to experience things while I've got the chance, before I go back."

"Yeah? Well, how about a little skydiving next? All you gotta do there is fall, and we both be fine at that."

"How about sailing?"

"You got a boat?"

"Didn't bring it with me. Come on, let's go around one more time. I'm getting the hang of it."

"Tell you what—you go around and I'll watch. I'm just gettin' the hang of hanging on here."

"Next couple of days, let's find a boat and go sailing."

"Only one I know that can sail is Molly."

"Oh, really? Imagine that. Where's she keep her boat?"

"She ain't got no boat, turkey. She's just like everybody else—she *knows* people that got boats. You gonna play that gig at Venice Blues tomorrow?"

"Sure."

"Well then, let's roll on outta here. We need some recovery time."

Chapter 7

"I handed in my thesis two weeks ago, Yuss. They want to publish it."

"That's big news! You must be proud as hell!"

"I was very proud. Some of the faculty took me out. We had a party. It was very nice."

"But Riv, you didn't even tell me."

"Would you have come? Would you have come to the celebration?"

"Well, maybe I couldn't have actually come, but at least—"

"To be honest, I missed you. But also to be honest, I realized that neither one of us seems to belong there at the other's important days. You remember, when I came there? Our ambitions, our plans, our celebrations are very different, Yussel. Our lives are different. So it's better this way."

"This way? *This way?* Are you saying that it's over? Just like that, on the telephone?"

"Don't be so dramatic, Yuss. It's difficult enough without that. Facing reality is always difficult. Saying it's over is just words. Our lives have become very different. We're not twenty years old anymore. We're not together anymore. I have thought about it a lot, and I don't think anybody's to blame for that. I used to think it was your fault, that you had changed. But we both have changed. It's not wrong. Who's to judge? Let God do that. I'm still very fond of you, Yuss—I love you, just in a different way. I want you to be happy. I want to be happy too. I think we will be happy living the kinds of lives we want to live."

"I don't feel very happy."

"Neither do I, right now. That's natural for both of us. But there's no need for a wailing and gnashing of teeth. This is not a disaster, just a difficult time of adjustment. We'll both be better off."

"Easy for you to say."

"No, very hard. But true. Or at least honest, as honest as I can be with myself and you. What we've had together we'll always have, that's not lost. And maybe you'll go on to be a big star. Maybe I'll become a best-selling author!" She laughed lightly. "It's possible, you know."

"You're very talented, Riv. And you work so hard. You're a terrific lady."

"Thank you."

"Being sarcastic?"

"No, not at all. I mean it. Those are nice compliments, and I know you mean them, and I feel very good hearing you say that. And while I haven't always understood what you were trying to do, and why, I think I understand it better now. I recognize how hard you work and how good you are. You're quite a fellow yourself."

"So I'm not chopped liver."

"Now you're being sarcastic."

"I'm sorry. This whole thing has just caught me by surprise."

"Only because maybe you haven't had as much time to think about it as I have. You've been so busy with other people. But I believe deep down we feel the same way. Somebody's at the door, Yuss. That'll be the messenger. I have to address an envelope for my revisions to the manuscript and give it to him."

"But can we talk later?"

"Of course. But first, Yuss, accept. Okay? Think about it and you'll see it's right. Then when we talk, we can talk about how we're doing, and be proud of each other, and it'll be much easier."

"I'll try. Bye, Riv."

"Shalom, Yussel."

What was most difficult to accept was that Rivka
was right, and the more right she was, the more respect
Jess had for her; the more respect he had for her, the
more valuable a woman she was; the more valuable
she was, the more of a loss it was to lose her.

That was the irony. And not a pleasant one. At
the same time, he felt a kind of relief—not that they
had split, but that the matter that had been disturbing
him had finally been brought out and decided. The
idea of it was not so hard as the finality. "It's
over."

But again she was right. That was a dramatic
phrase, like a stage line, the saying or even thinking of
which was not necessary. The main ingredients of their
relationship had been diminished for some time. The
world in which Rivka strove, in which she wanted to
stay, in which she aspired to succeed, was not his
world.

It made it easier that she had stopped blaming
him for their differences. Because then he could stop
blaming himself. There was guilt enough to go around
as it was. The world was full of guilt. Guilt and
atonement, guilt and atonement, but there was never
atonement enough. What you had to do was live. You
had to live your own life as best you could, according
to the best standards you could apply and hope to
meet.

Sometimes he felt his own way was cheaper, less
meaningful, and hers more important, more worthy.
But so much of that was in his upbringing—the same
for everybody. Who's to judge? Let God judge, just as
she said. Maybe his gift—his atonement, perhaps—
was in providing people simple pleasures in music.
Thousands, maybe millions of people.

Not so bad a gift, not so small an atonement, not
so common a calling.

For the next several days, he didn't feel so good
about himself. But that was mainly because Rivka had
faced the reality sooner and been the one to present it
to him. He could accept it, in time. And when other
tests came, maybe he would face reality sooner. He
was not a man to hurt people, not a man to shirk his

responsibilities, not a man to quit in difficult circumstances.

He felt good about what she had said: "You're quite a fellow yourself." She wouldn't have said it if she didn't mean it. He would make it true.

The Venice Blues Club was packed and responsive, as usual. He gave them "You, Baby" and "Amazed and Confused," upbeat and easy to pull off. But when he turned to the ballads, like "Love on the Rocks" and "Songs of Life," which required more (as Bubba put it) "soul and control," something was missing.

Maybe the audience didn't notice, but the ballads weren't right. The beat seemed to drag, he couldn't quite get his voice loose, couldn't get the phrasing to flow. The intensity, the fine meshing of voice and guitar, the deftly placed stresses and subtle pauses—those things that gave him power in his songs—were lacking.

"Let's pick it up a little," Jess said to Bubba during an instrumental riff between verses.

Bubba raised his eyebrows. "You sure?"

Jess nodded, waited a moment while they synced the quicker beat, then turned back to the mike and picked up the verse: "Oh, and when the moment's true . . . It sings so softly to me and you . . . You know it's true . . . You know it's true."

It still wasn't right. It wasn't the beat, it was his voice. It was a nuance probably nobody else would notice. Jess felt like he was plowing through the song rather than riding the wave of it. The more he thought, the worse it got. Finally he finished, then he knew what it was.

Offstage, Bubba put an arm around him. "What was that all about, my man? Picking up the beat. You in a hurry to get someplace?"

"Maybe. Something like that."

"Sounded fine to me, the way it was."

"Concentration, Bubba. That's what was wrong. My mind's running off every which way, I'm not into the songs. And I'm trying to force it."

"That a fact? Well, you wrote the line for it: 'Everything I tried to touch with softness has broken into bits too small to see.' Like your head is all busted up, too many things in there flyin' around like birds in a living room—birds come in a window, suddenly don't know where they're at, what's comin' down, what they're supposed to do, don't know how to get out. Just know they're birds, that's all. Thoughts come in like that sometimes—don't belong there, can't get out, can't settle down, got to fly. So they just bang around in your noggin drivin' you nuts."

"Something like that."

"Well, it was fine anyway. Folks loved it just like always. Only one bothered was you."

"That's enough."

"Well, you're right there. You get too deep into that, you'll start to lose your confidence. And that's the worst thing that can happen."

"I know."

"So, my man, you gotta get your head cleaned up."

"Yup."

The marina was blindingly bright. White-hulled powerboats, glistening teak decks, multicolored sails being raised and lowered. Tanned people walking around in blue jeans or shorts and T-shirts and white deck sneakers. The calm blue water lapped against the pilings and hulls like the pat of after-shave lotion being applied.

The first thing that struck Jess was the brilliant beauty of it all. The second thing was the mystery and the freedom of travel. The third was money. So much money here. How could so many people have so much money just to buy pleasure boats?

He felt envious and out of place, like an urchin peering through the gates at a garden party. The names on the sterns of the boats spoke of love and exotic places: *Emily II; My Fair Sadie; Cape Sarafan; Zophistal.*

He didn't know where to look, so he just wandered as casually as possible, looking intently while trying not to gape, afraid that at any moment some-body would ask him who he was and what business he had being there.

He found himself staring at a rear end over which blue jeans were stretched tight on a woman bent over a paint pail. She was on the foredeck of what seemed to Jess an enormous cabin cruiser. When she straightened up and turned, it was to apply some brush strokes to the ventilator hood that protruded from the deck. He watched her because there was something attractive in how she was dressed—blue bandanna on her head, a loose, paint-stained man's shirt—and something vague-ly familiar in her movements.

When she paused in her work to draw the back of a hand over her cheek and gaze off at some other boats, he recognized her. He did not recognize the man who joined her, coming out of the cabin to examine her work. The man, bare chested, was blond and very well tanned, a goddamned Adonis.

Jess waited for the man to walk away. Then he stuffed his fingers into his pants pockets and strolled along the dock toward the boat. When he was close enough to speak without shouting he said, "You're a hard lady to track down."

Molly quickly turned, stood awkwardly for a mo-ment dangling her paintbrush. "What are you doing here?"

"Looking for you." He stood next to the boat and looked up at her.

She put the brush down and came over to the rail. "Eddie Gibbs told me you were signing the record deal this morning."

"I've been calling for the last three days. I'm tired of talking to your answering service."

"They didn't give me any message."

"I didn't leave any."

"Then you can hardly blame me for——"

"Like talking to that damn clown-face at the fast-food place."

"An answering service is so that people who want to reach me *can* reach me."

"What are you doing here?"

"I asked you first."

"And I told you—I was looking for you."

"I, um, we're getting the boat ready." She gestured toward the cabin. "Tommy asked me to go to, unh, Acapulco with him. So we're getting ready to leave."

"Acapulco?" Jess felt his heart sink.

"Yes, that's right." She nodded briskly. "Acapulco. Something wrong with that?"

"No, of course not."

She leaned over the gleaming steel rail. "Look, Jess, if you've got a problem with the record deal, talk to Eddie. I've told you, he's the best agent in town for that."

"The deal's fine. It's got nothing to do with the deal." He looked around, scuffed his foot on the wooden planking of the deck, then looked back at her. "I just want to talk to you."

"So talk."

Jess shifted uneasily. "You make it so difficult . . ."

"What's difficult?" She spread her arms innocently. "You want to talk, I'm standing here listening."

"Well . . . look . . . what I'm trying to say is . . . hey, couldn't we have a cup of coffee or something?"

"I got paint all over myself."

"Maybe lunch a little later, or dinner."

She pondered, looking off over the boats, avoiding his eyes. "Look, I don't think so, Jess. I showed you around, maybe opened a few doors for you. Now you're on your way and I'm taking a little vacation." Now she looked at him. "Okay?"

"What about our contract?"

She chuckled mirthlessly. "Short term, we both fulfilled our obligations. You need any help in the future, you can count on me."

"But why can't . . . why don't . . ."

Tommy emerged from the cabin and came over. "We've got company," he said, not unfriendly.

"Tommy," Molly extended a hand toward Jess, "this is Jess Robin. He's a new singer. A terrific singer."

"Really? Well, it's a pleasure." He reached down over the rail to shake Jess' hand. "Glad to meet you, Jess. Come aboard. Have a beer. Let me show you around."

"Unh, no thanks. I'm kind of in a hurry."

"Well, any time. Hope to see your name in lights. Looks good up here, Molly," he eyed her work. "When you're finished, you can help me aft with the trim."

"Be there in a minute."

They both watched him walk away.

Jess envied the way he seemed so at home on the boat, so in command. He envied him so hard his head ached. "He seems like a nice guy."

"Yeah, he is." Molly nodded. "Real nice guy."

"Well, that's good."

"Yup. So you're in a hurry."

"Yeah, kind of."

"Good luck, Rabinovitch." She reached her hand down.

He took her hand lightly. "Sure, right."

"So." She withdrew her hand and half-turned away.

"So, well, thanks for everything."

"Don't mention it."

"And have fun in Acapulco."

"Sure."

Jess gave her a little wave and started slowly walking away on the dock. He walked slower and slower. He stopped. He started walking again quickly, then stopped again. He realized that the only reason he was walking away was because he didn't want to make a fool out of himself; the reason he was stopping was because walking away would make him a bigger fool.

At last he turned and, with the bearing and determination of a General Patton, marched back to the boat. Molly was back at work.

"Molly!"

She snapped her head around.

"Not a damn word until I've finished!"

She stared at him, momentarily flustering him by the silence he demanded.

"Okay! Now listen. See, well, you know Rivka

went back to New York right after I sang the other
night. And since then we talked. And we got some
things straight. We just don't want the same things
anymore. There's nothing wrong with that, see? Nobody's to blame. It's just facing reality. And we decided it's over between us. Understand?"

"I'm really sorry to hear—"

"I'm not finished! So we're splitting up. No big
deal, it happens every day. And I'm not looking for
sympathy or anything like that. I'm fine. She's fine too.
We're all fine."

"That's fine." She couldn't resist it, though she
concealed her smile.

Jess waggled his hand as if erasing a blackboard.
"But what I mean is, what I wanted to tell you is . . .
well, listen. While we were working together, hanging
out together, it was, I got to feel, you know, like it
was . . ." His voice trailed off in confusion.

She feigned a sigh. "Jess, whatever you're trying
to say, why don't you just say it?"

"Well, damn it, what I'm trying to say is that I
don't want you to go to Acapulco!"

"That so?" She cocked her head.

"You're laughing at me."

"Smiling. I'm not used to taking orders."

"It's not an order!"

"Oh?"

He cleared his throat and lowered his voice. "It's
a request. I don't want you to go to Acapulco . . . with
him."

She nodded slowly. "I see."

"You don't see."

"Ah, well, I've had bigger disappointments." She
cupped a hand at the side of her mouth and called
toward the cagin, "Hey, Tommy?"

"Yeah, babe?" He poked his head out.

"Would you mind very much if I didn't go to
Acapulco with you?"

"Acapulco? Who the hell's going to Acapulco?
You think the owners would let me take this thing to
Acapulco? We're just going to cruise around Catalina
for the day, little shakedown cruise. You want to go to

Acapulco, find somebody who owns his own boat and has time to play. Jesus!" He went back inside.

"Uh-oh." Molly looked at Jess out of the corner of her eye.

He was already advancing up the gangplank, wagging his finger at her.

"Uh-oh." She began backing away.

"Yeah, yeah, I'm gonna get you for that." He eyed her fiercely, chuckling. "You're gonna pay, Molly Oliver."

"I thought you'd enjoy a little joke." She slid behind the ventilator. "Just a joke."

"Ho, ho, ho!" He came after her in a crouch. "And for the punch line, you're gonna do a little running. You're going to run until you're clear off the dock."

"Jess, you can't make me do that." She edged around the duct as he stalked her.

"Or else you're going straight into the Pacific Ocean or whatever it is in here."

"No."

"Yes!" He leaped for her.

She scampered away, ran down the gangplank, and raced off the dock.

Jess trotted after her, glorying in the voice he heard behind him:

"Molly? Molly, where are you? Molly? . . ."

"Come on, on your feet, you!"

"I can't." Jess lay on his belly in the sand, gasping. "I can't run anymore, we'll never get that thing up."

"On your feet, buster!" Molly grabbed him under an arm. "You screwed up my vacation, kept me from going to Acapulco, so now we're going to have *fun*."

He struggled to his feet and took the kite from her and began wearily trotting into the wind, holding the kite up behind him. "I thought . . . we were gonna talk."

She slogged along behind him, waving her arms up to urge the kite into the air. "Every time we stop to talk, you can't think of anything to say."

"All I want to say is—"

"Keep running!"

"All . . . I want . . . to say is—"

"It's going! It's going up! Let out some string!"

He let the string spin off the reel, still keeping his feet plodding through the sand at the edge of the water.

"Stop! Just let the string out, fast!"

He stopped and turned, feeling the reel spin crazily in his hands. The kite was drifting up, wiggling like a fish trying to shake a lure. More string spun out. The kite rose more smoothly. Finally it was soaring, making huge swoops against the sky.

"There. Let's sit down and watch it."

"Whew." Jess dropped into the sand.

"You're gonna get a sunburn."

"Really?" He looked at his bare chest.

"Well, maybe not. You've got dark skin. You've never been sunburned?"

"I hardly ever went to the beach."

"What's the matter? Atlantic's not good enough for you?"

"It's such a hassle in New York. Subways, buses, carrying everything. Not worth it. I can't believe I'm so out of shape."

"You don't look out of shape."

"I never get fat or anything. I used to run. I even used to take fencing lessons. Fencing's great exercise."

"You some kind of Douglas Fairbanks, Jr.?"

"Yeah. Watch for my next movie. Great duel scenes."

She watched the kite, shielding her eyes with a hand. "So, Jess, you were saying?"

"Saying what?"

"My question exactly. Now's a good time to talk."

He took a couple of deep breaths. "All I wanted to say is, let's spend the day together."

"Well, for chrissake, what do you think we've been doing? We skated, we rode bikes, now we're flying a kite. What more do you want? We didn't get started until noon, when you chased me off that boat."

"I know. But that's all I wanted to say."

"That's all?"

"Well, what are you doing for supper?"

"Staying home. I feel like cooking. Just for myself and a guest."

"Oh." He quickly took his eyes off her and stared blindly at the kite.

"You aren't much of a skater."

"I know."

"Or a bike rider either, for that matter."

"I forgot how."

"You never forget how to ride a bike. You like my T-shirt?"

Her white T-shirt, which fitted her snugly and enticingly, bore the message: GO FOR IT!

He nodded without looking at her. "Yeah, I do."

"Good. What are you doing for supper?"

"Hunh?"

She put a hand to her forehead. "What a bozo. Listen, if you're going to be my guest, I might as well know what you like."

"Oh, me?"

"You got other plans?"

"No. Anything. Whatever you like to fix."

"Good. I'll surprise you. You can rest up while I shop."

He fell asleep in Molly's spare bedroom, and awoke to the touch of her hand on his shoulder, and the smells of a good meal cooking—sweet, strong, undefinable but oven-rich.

"You hungry?" she asked. "Everything's ready."

He sat up and rubbed his eyes.

"Come on." She beckoned him.

The dining table had been set rather formally, with blue-flowered plates, heavy silverware, sparkling wine glasses, and two candles in silver sticks. He sat down while she went to the kitchen. He heard the oven door squeak open, then shortly bang shut.

Molly came in proudly bearing a serving platter on which sat a steaming ham, studded with cloves and surrounded by rings of pineapple. She put it in the center of the table and stood back to smile at him.

He stared at the platter.

"What's the matter?" she asked.

"Nothing." He tried to smile.

"Ohmygod." She put a hand to her mouth. "Ham! I forgot!"

"It's okay, I'm not all that religious."

"Forget it. I'm not going to be the one that leads you onto the path of uncleanliness." She snatched up the platter and carried it back to the kitchen, calling, "Anyway, it'll keep."

"We could eat it, Molly, really." He felt awful.

"You ever eat ham?"

"No."

"It'll make you go blind." She came back in, smiling brightly.

"After all you did."

"What? Stick a ham in the oven? Nothing. Anyway, now we'll go with one of the better all-purpose substitutes."

"What's that?"

"How you feel about pizza?"

"Hungry."

"Grab your coat, let's go."

They drove to the little red-and-white building to pick up their pizza dinners, then parked on a bluff overlooking the ocean to eat.

"I'm really sorry about this," Jess said.

"You are? I'm not. I love this garbage."

"Well, so do I, as a matter of fact."

"It was dumb of me, forgetting about things like ham."

"Religion has its dumb rules."

"That isn't the way I feel about it. I respect things like that."

"You do?"

"Sure. If nothing else, it gives you some discipline. It's like Catholics not eating meat on Fridays. It's really a discipline thing more than anything else, not a question of sin."

"Is that so?"

"Yup."

"You're Catholic?"

"I'm not religious either. But born and raised, yes. And so I have the habit of eating fish on Fridays. No big deal, but why not?"

"I feel better already." He licked his fingers. "So you don't think religion's crazy?"

"Of course not. I respect just about anybody who believes in anything. It's *not* believing in anything that drives me up the wall. It's such a cop-out. That doesn't mean you have to be religious, exactly. But some kind of moral ethic, that's important. People who don't believe in anything are just avoiding any discipline, more often than not."

"A philosopher, yet."

"Speaking of discipline, I think we just finished the whole pizza." Molly started gathering the greasy napkins and tossed them into the empty box.

"You in a hurry to get home?"

"No. Why?"

"Something I'd like to show you."

"Fine."

He had noticed it on the way to the pizza joint, and now he directed her back to it: a pleasant little gray synagogue on a nice, quiet street. They parked and went in.

In the foyer, Jess was given a silken black yarmulke which he patted into place on his thick hair. Molly tied on her blue bandanna. They took a seat in the rear.

It pleased him how she followed the service, finding the pages in the prayer book as the rabbi directed, listening rapt to the cantor, and even closing her eyes through some of the more beautiful passages.

When the service was over and they came out, Molly said simply, "Thank you."

Back at the house, he pulled her gently to him and kissed her on the lips.

"You taste of pizza," she said.

"Sorry."

"No." She pressed her lips to his again, holding the kiss, putting her arms slowly around him. "Stay," she said.

"Okay."

They undressed each other slowly, carefully, savoring the moment. Jess had never been undressed by a woman, or undressed one, and he wondered at her practiced hands and tried not to be clumsy with his own. But his discomfort was fleeting, she made him comfortable.

"You're beautiful," he said.

"You too."

"Thank you."

"No, we don't have to say that." She eased him down onto the bed. "That can become interminable. Let's just take it for granted that we appreciate each other."

And he was glad he didn't have to thank her, because it would have become interminable, for the pleasures she gave him, and for those he obviously gave her.

Jess expected to feel guilty, but didn't. He felt primarily peaceful, warm, appreciated. He feared that their parting in the morning would be awkward, but it wasn't. It was taken for granted, as was the fact that he would return.

"Later," she said at the door, blowing him a kiss.

"Later."

She had offered him a ride to Bubba's, but he wanted to walk for a while. He hadn't felt so light in some time, maybe never. It seemed impossible, the turns his life took, the rapid swings lately, the failures and successes and gains and losses. He didn't know if he could trust any of it. He was afraid something lay out there in ambush for him, something sinister or ordinary that would bring him back to reality—whatever that was, which was something he couldn't reckon with certainty any more.

Whatever misfortune might be lurking for the future, it was all swept aside in his mind by thoughts of

Molly and the good fortune that seemed to make up the present.

He was buoyant until he reached Bubba's apartment. Then he suddenly got nervous because he didn't know what to say about any of this.

Bubba was sitting on the sofa, gnawing on a chicken bone from a box, and leafing through a copy of the *Hollywood Reporter*.

"Hey, my man, welcome home." Bubba glanced up, then returned to his newspaper.

"Hey." Jess waited for the questions, but they didn't come. Bubba had taste.

"Eddie Gibbs is looking for you."

"Problems?"

"Didn't say. Didn't sound like it. Just wanted to make sure you gonna show up for the recording session, be ready, this, that, and the other."

"I'll be ready."

"I know."

"I've got a few days."

"I know that too. You gonna finish that song?"

"I got it about done, in my head. Where's everybody?" Jess went to the kitchen and opened a beer.

"Where they supposed to be—working, playing, whatever."

"Something bothering you, Bubba?"

"Something should be?" He kept reading.

"I stayed with Molly."

"I figured either that or you was in a ditch some place."

"You worried about me?" Jess had a warm feeling for Bubba.

"Just like to know things going your way, my man. You wasn't in too good a frame of mind when you left here yesterday."

"I should've given you a call."

"However you want to play it."

"I guess I've been a little wrapped up in myself lately, Bubba."

"You'll get over it. You ain't the kind to forget your friends. And tell you something else, my man—I ain't easy to ditch."

"You're terrific, Bubba."

"Know how you can make it up to me? Sing that new song."

"You got it. Get some drumsticks and give me some rhythm."

"Think I'll just use these here two from this box."

And so Jess got out his guitar, and Bubba wrapped napkins around the chicken legs. With Bubba drumming on the newspaper, Jess sang "Hello Again," adding new lines:

"Hello my friend, hello . . . Just called to let you know . . . I think about you every night . . . When I'm here alone . . . And you're there at home . . . Hello."

The dinner table was set with Sabbath candles, unlit. Jess and Molly stood at the window, holding hands, watching the sun go down. It formed a glowing arc on the far rim of the Pacific, then sank away, loosing streamers of pastel beams that glowed like neon across the water and up into the pale sky.

Then they turned to the table. It was what Molly most wanted to do this Friday night, to have the Sabbath ritual in her bungalow.

Jess put the square of lace on Molly's hair, and she lit the candles. The light glinted off the glazed, braided hallah bread and the goblets of wine. Jess bent over the bread and wine and softly said the kiddush blessing. He lifted his goblet to sip the wine, then held it for Molly. She sipped, their eyes holding over the glass.

There was a reverence in the air Jess wanted not to disturb, an intimacy and warmth beyond the Sabbath ceremony.

Impulsively, he dipped his finger into the wine and brushed it over Molly's parted lips, tracing them in a caress. She lowered the glass and they leaned forward over it, gently bringing their lips together. The light taste of wine sealed their kiss like a dedication.

He whispered, "I love you, Molly."

It was the last night of the gig at the Venice Blues Club. Jess was as strong as he had ever been, and he had the audience in the palm of his hand from the opening number. The brothers had been lifted by Jess's spirit, and played with a freedom and zest they hadn't felt in a long time. So intensely was the crowd involved in the performance that business was bad; people weren't ordering, waiters couldn't get through. Everybody was on their feet after each song, cheering and begging for more.

Jess slipped off his guitar strap and provoked an immediate chorus of disappointed boos and optimistic calls for encores. He held up his hands to quiet them.

"Listen, folks," he called through the mike, "you've been terrific. And we're not quite done."

Cheers and hurrays burst through the room.

"But now I'd like to do something a little different. It's mostly a treat for us up here, if you don't mind. But I've been with these guys here and there, one way or another, for many years. And every little once in a while, it's fun to take a look back at where you've come from. So I'd like to show you. By the way, this is as much a surprise to the Brothers Four here as it is to you. But let's give it a shot."

Followed by the puzzled looks of Bubba and the brothers, Jess went to the rear of the stage and opened a trunk. He took out a set of bongos, a snare drum and sticks, a tambourine, a set of maracas, and a small brown paper bag. He passed them out—bongos to Timmy, snare and sticks to Bubba, the tambourine to Mel, and the bag to Teddy. Teddy laughed when he reached into the bag to take out a new comb and a box of tissue. The whole group took up the laughter.

Jess returned to the mike, carrying the maracas. "So folks, here is the way we got started, just how we used to sound on the street corners in New York City. May I present to you the Big Apple Blues Blowers!"

He waved dramatically to the brothers, Bubba set the beat, and they were off—the gay primitive sounds from the pass-the-hat days, Jess singing the lead to a happy rendition of the "St. Louis Blues":

"I hate to see the evenin' sun go down . . ."

They went through verse after verse, more and more of the crowd joining in, until they were drained of energy. Nickels and dimes came sailing up onto the stage.

Finally they put their makeshift instruments aside, and while the crowd was still roaring, Bubba came up to Jess.

"My man, let's really give them a treat to wrap it up."

"What you got in mind, Bubba?"

"Let's give them a taste of the brand-new song before you cut that side. They been good to you, Jess."

A smile gradually spread over Jess's face. "Yeah! What the hell? We might as well find out right now whether it works or not."

It worked. The audience, so energetic before, singing and dancing in the aisles for the music of the Big Apple Blues Blowers, now listened with rapt silence while Jess sang his newly completed ballad, "Hello Again."

Chapter 8

It took a lot of thinking, even though Molly made it sound simple and normal and comfortable. But it was not simple or normal for Jess. It was exciting and crazy. Everything was crazy lately, everything was moving too fast. Things happening to his life made him feel out of control. And yet, it was marvelous, all of it. If only, as Molly persistently suggested, he could relax and ride with it.

He poured a second cup of coffee and brought it into the living room and put it in front of Bubba, who had gotten out of bed a few minutes before, reached the sofa, leaned back, and immediately fallen asleep again.

"Bubba?"

"Hunh?" Bubba's head snapped up.

"What would you think if I moved out?"

Bubba blinked and shook his head, trying to rouse himself. "Come again?"

"If I moved out, how bad an idea would that be?"

"This my coffee here?"

"Yeah."

Bubba took some sips and put the cup down. "Whooee, these hours are gettin' to me. Hey, that's a good line. Even rhymes. Why don't you write it down?"

"Be serious for a minute."

"I'm serious as a heart attack, bro. I need more sleep. Playin' those fine gigs, partying afterward, little too much of this, little too much of that. Things going too good for this old body of mine."

"Get in a little late last night?"

"Well now," Bubba smiled wryly, "that's something you wouldn't know, right? Since I don't guess you were here yourself until lately."

"That's what I'm talking about."

Bubba rubbed his eyes. "Do me a favor, make some sense."

"Start over?"

"From the top."

"What would you think if I moved out?"

"Moved out."

"Yeah."

"Mmm." Bubba sipped his coffee and leaned back, folding his hands behind his head. "Well, since I don't guess you mean move out and sleep in the dirt, I guess you mean you would move *in* someplace else."

"Yeah."

"Well then, the main thing is where you moving *into*, and how would I feel about that. Since I don't need you here except to make coffee and wake me up ten times a day."

"Okay, how would you feel about it?"

"She ask you?"

"Sort of."

"Sort of! Whooo! Sort of don't mean diddly, in the move-in business."

"What I mean is, we just kind of got around to it, without any formal request or anything."

"So everything's already agreed to."

"I guess."

"What're you so damn worried about?" Bubba got up and began stomping around the room in circles like an old bull turning a grinding wheel. "You don't have to take a poll, my man. Just be cool. You got to learn to just get down with stuff. Ain't nothing means forever. Like they say all the time out here, go with the flow. Quit worrying everything to death. Ain't nothing certain but death and Texas. Do what you feel like, what makes you feel good."

"Taxes."

"What?"

"Taxes. It's death and *taxes*."

"I don't care if it's birth and bird poop. You know what I mean. You gotta get over the idea that everything that goes good and feels good is bad news."

"I'm working on it."

Bubba stopped in front of him and smiled wide. "Well, sounds to me like you're working on it pretty good. Just don't go mistreating that lady. I'll put you on a pair of roller skates and send you straight off the Santa Monica pier!"

"Why would I mistreat her? I love her, Bubba."

Bubba chuckled and shook his head. "I swear, Jess, some days you sound whiter than other days."

Jess laughed. "You don't like love talk."

Bubba winced. Without opening his eyes, he said, "Do me a favor and just have a good time. 'Fore you lose all the black I tried to pump into you all these years. You got that album to cut. Then we got the TV gig with Zany Gray. I don't want you out there sounding like some lovesick Robert Goulet."

"How've I been sounding lately?"

Bubba clamped a hand on his shoulder. "Just lately, my man, you been sounding steady and ready. You got the groove. You ain't never been better."

Jess grinned and leaned back, sighing with satisfaction. "What a life. You've really been something for me, Bubba."

"Yeah, well don't send me no flowers. You better get a move on, turkey, you gonna do what you have to do and get to the studio on time."

Jess changed clothes at Molly's, then sat down at the piano to go over the music one more time. He wondered how many times he'd been through this song, how many changes he'd made from the beginning, why it was impossible to make it perfect. He changed one note, moving E to G, played the song through, and changed it back. He looked at his watch. "Molly?"

He went through the house, looking for her, then went to the front door.

Down at the curb, Molly, in the same paint-spattered man's shirt she had been wearing to paint the boat, was painting the mailbox.

He trotted down to her.

"How you like it?" She stepped back proudly, wiping her hands with a rag.

Next to her name was now his: "Molly Oliver—Jess Robin."

"Make you nervous? Hunh?" She gave him a hug, nuzzling his shoulder.

"What makes me nervous is we're gonna be late. It's beautiful. Get your clothes changed."

She scampered inside. He stood there eyeing the mailbox. It was beautiful. Just a touch would make it perfect. He dipped the brush into the can and drew a little heart under the names. He pondered that for a moment, grimaced, snatched up the rag, and wiped it off. "All I would need was for Bubba to see that," he mumbled.

At the recording studio, the music was passed out. The musicians—a real orchestra of strings, wood-winds, brass, percussion—noodled with it, then went through it once together. Barney Callahan, in charge of it all, prowled around restlessly.

Finally they were ready. Jess donned his headset and stepped to the microphone. Molly and Barney went into the control booth. The technician signaled, Jess gave the downbeat, and they began recording "Hello Again."

After a few bars, they stopped. The orchestra leader walked over to the string section and gave some instructions.

They began again. After a few bars, Jess waved them to stop and pulled off his headset. "Sorry, but I'm not feeling the beat enough. It's a ballad, but it needs a more solid beat to keep it from being soppy."

Twice more they began, twice more they stopped, once for Jess to correct the string section on the precise manner he wanted them to come in, once because he felt his own note had not been solid enough.

On the next time, they went through the whole song. Barney came out of the booth. "Sounded marvelous, Mr. Robin, just marvelous."

Jess nodded thoughtfully. "Let's do it again. I didn't finish right."

Barney pursed his lips, glanced at his watch, and nodded at the orchestra leader, then went back to the booth.

Jess gave Molly a wink, she winked back from the booth. He was very glad she was there. If she had not been there, Jess wouldn't have felt confident enough to call for all these replays, to insist on the precision he felt was crucial. But she seemed not at all nervous about it, and he took his cue from her.

From the intercom came Barney's voice: "Ready, Mr. Robin?"

"Ready."

Barney raised his finger. The technician announced, "Roll tape, 'Hello Again,' take five."

This was it, Jess felt it now. The orchestra was rich and full behind him, the strings came in just right, giving him the lift he loved from a string section, his phrasing flowed.

In the booth, Molly whispered instructions to the technicians working the console as they adjusted pot levels, flipped switches, pushed buttons.

Jess hit the last notes of the song, just the way he wanted them:

"But I couldn't wait . . . Hello."

Barney's voice boomed through the intercom. "Beautiful! That's a keeper! Right, Mr. Robin?"

"You got it!" Jess happily laid aside his headset and nodded appreciatively to the orchestra. The answering smiles all around told him it was right.

He looked up at the booth, saw Molly blow him a kiss and mouth "I love you."

He returned the kiss and mouthed back silently, "I love you too."

Everybody shuffled music around to prepare for the next song.

A taxi pulled up and out of it Cantor Rabinovitch stepped cautiously. He tottered for a second, getting his bearings, and squinted through his thick glasses into the morning glare. He was carrying a small, worn suitcase that hung heavily on his arm. He watched the taxi pull away, then looked over at the bungalow.

He walked to the door and leaned close to see the number, checked it against the address on an envelope in his hand, then stared at the door before slowly raising his finger to the bell.

It took a while for Jess to pull on his jeans and sweatshirt and pad barefoot to the door. When he opened it, he gasped.

"Papa!"

His father stood imperturbably, looking him up and down. "They don't have shoes in California?"

"Papa!" Jess threw his arms around him and rocked him back and forth.

"What are you doing here? Why didn't you call? I would have met you at the airport. What a fantastic surprise to see you!"

"Why call?" His father lightly disengaged himself. "I'm here. Aren't you going to invite an old man in?"

"Please!" Jess stepped back and held the door wide for his father to pass.

He took a look back outside. "No gondolas—they call this Venice?"

"The whole Pacific Ocean, Papa. Isn't that enough?"

"Who knows where people get names?" His father let the door be closed behind him and scanned the room. "Even Robin."

"Come on, Papa. Let me take this." Jess removed the bag from his father's hand and put it beside the sofa. "I can't believe you're here. Sit down." He held his father's elbow while the man slowly lowered himself onto the cushions.

"Belief comes with age, my son, like faith, maybe." He craned his neck a little to see down the hall.

"Nobody else is here, Papa, just us."

"Ah."

"Can I get you a cup of tea? Something to eat?"

"Tea would be nice. I ate on the plane. They don't let you stop eating."

"I know." Jess chuckled. "Isn't it great, flying over the country?"

"It's a big country."

"I'll get the tea." He headed for the kitchen, still talking. "You're dressed very warm, Papa, for here. Aren't you warm?"

"I don't have clothes for all the climates of the world, Yussel. I am comfortable."

"It's a nice place here, isn't it? See the piano? That's where I do my work, you know, composing and practicing. Want to try it?"

"What would I try?" He shrugged. "I have my own piano."

"Come on, Papa, try it. It's a good one."

He heaved a sigh of resignation and hoisted himself wearily from the sofa and went over to sit down at the piano. He leaned forward to peer at the trademark. "Yamaha. Who makes a Yamaha?"

"The Japanese make wonderful pianos, Papa. That company also makes motorcycles."

"Ah. Music and speed. Something for everybody. Steinway should make a motorcycle." He began to pick out a melody delicately with just one finger. Five notes, repeated several times.

Jess came into the living room carrying two tea cups and singing softly with the melody: "My name is Yussel . . . My name is Yussel."

"You remember."

"I remember." He sang, "Noah built the Ark . . . yes, Noah built the Ark . . ."

They sang the next line together: "For the Lord said, 'Build! Build!' "

The cantor sang alone: "For the Lord said . . ."

And Jess finished: " 'Build! Build! Build!' "

"So." He turned to Jess. "Some things you remember."

"Sit on the sofa, Papa, for your tea. Everything you taught me, I remember."

"Everything?" He arranged himself properly on

the sofa and lifted the tea bag from the cup and let it
drip.

"Papa." Jess sat next to him and put an arm
around the sloping shoulders. "It's so good to see you.
So much has happened."

"You look good, Yussel, for someone who's
changed so much."

"I haven't changed so much, Papa."

"You haven't?" He looked at Jess, his chin pulled
back. Then he looked demonstratively around the
room. "For someone who hasn't changed so much . . ."

"Papa, you always said seasons change, people
don't."

"Maybe I was wrong, you're the exception."

"No. Some things in my life have changed, like
seasons, but I'm the same. I'm still your son."

His father sat stiffly erect, his hands on his knees,
facing directly forward, and said in measured cadence,
"Then come home with me now."

Jess looked away. "I can't."

"Can't? Someone owns you here? You're on a
chain? You're behind a fence like Auschwitz?"

"No, Papa, not like that. I just cut my first album,
and—"

"I read your letter. I know."

"And I've also got a spot coming up on Zany
Gray's TV show."

"For cameras, you sing now."

"Look, Papa," Jess put a hand on his shoulder, "I
know it's hard for you to understand, but I'm starting
a whole new career. It's what I have to do because I
have to be true to myself."

"Yourself first, and not your God?"

"It's not like that. But God gave me a talent, and
he gave me feelings, and that's why I sing."

"I know about singing, Yussel. I know how you
sing. You can sing beautifully, from the heart. You're
a cantor."

"Papa, the world will get along without another
cantor."

"You make a pronouncement on what the world

can get along without? Our little congregation, the world could get along without that too? Or why not Jews altogether? Some have believed the world would be well rid of Jews. And now I hear my son talk about what the world can get along without. A son knows more than God."

"That's not what I meant, Papa, you know that. It's just that there are other things I—"

"No!" He pushed the teacup away. "Ask yourself, Yussel, why, when so many died in the war, why did God spare us—a family of cantors?"

"Papa . . ."

"You think there is no reason? You think the world could get along just as well without us? Yet we were spared. Ask yourself."

"Papa, I have asked myself . . ."

"To sing in shul! That is the reason we were spared. To serve Him!"

"Other Jews were spared, they do other things. And sons, and sons of sons, they do different things from their fathers."

"Cantors! For five generations, we are cantors. There is a meaning in that, sense to it. It is not nonsense. You think it is nonsense, Yussel?"

"No, not nonsense." Jess hated to see his father becoming so upset, and wished there were a way to calm him, to ease his mind. But at the same time he felt his own tension rising. He struggled for composure.

"Words." His father made fists on his knees. "We are playing with words. There is no time for that. You are my son?" He turned slowly, like a robot, to face him. "Yussel, come home with me now, before it's too late! Before you betray everything you were born to be!" He rose from the sofa. "If you are my son, you will—"

"Stop it, Papa!" Jess jumped to his feet to face him. "Stop it! For once in your life you're going to listen to me. I know that's what you believe—and I've tried to live up to that. But I can't anymore. I just can't. There are things inside of me—songs, feelings,

ideas I've got to express. Maybe they come from God
too, I don't know. But I do know that I have to find
my own way!"

The cantor listened to his outburst with calmly
raised eyebrows. "Your own way," he repeated, mus-
ing. "For that you desert your synagogue, your God,
your wife . . ."

"That's not fair!"

"It's not true, perhaps?"

The old man's calm, firm words now unsettled
Jess, as had the man's impassioned words before. "I'm
not deserting anybody. And certainly not Rivka. We
have *both* decided to get a divorce, to go our own
ways."

"So simple . . ."

"People break up every day."

"What people do every day is not justification for
a cantor, or for a cantor's son, or for you! I will not
listen to it!"

His father's renewed flare of anger, making his
face as stern as an unforgiving god, caused Jess to take
a step backward.

Just then the front door swung open, and Molly
came in carrying a full bag of groceries, saying, "Dar-
ling, there's another bag in the car. Would you
mind—" She saw his father and stopped dead in her
tracks.

Jess rushed to her as to a savior, and put an arm
around her, looking back at his father. "Papa, I want
you to meet Molly Oliver. Molly, this is my father."

Anger and anguish melded on the old man's face,
a look of such potent distress that it froze them in the
room, like stone statues. His voice rose slowly. "No . . .
no . . . I have no son."

The cantor grasped his jacket lapel with both
hands, tightening his grip on it as deliberately as a boa
gripping a victim. Then, with a ritualistic flourish, he
yanked his arm, ripping the lapel. And as the torn
lapel dangled incongruously, almost comically, from
his jacket, his voice rumbled as from the bowels of a
volcano:

"Baruch Dayan Emes!"

Then the old man moved, as if in a trance, past them through the open door.

Molly gaped, uncomprehending, at Jess. Jess was stunned, not breathing, dizzied by the words, and could not move at once.

Seconds passed. Suddenly Jess sprang to the door, calling, "Papa! No! Don't go! Don't leave me, Papa! Come back, please . . ." His voice trailed off to weeping and he leaned against the jamb for support.

Molly was at his side, watching the old man walk away with a heavy gait.

"I love you, Papa . . ." she heard Jess say in a choked voice, and she didn't know whether she should touch him or not. "Jess," she said very softly, trying not to startle him, "what happened? Can you tell me? What was all that about? Why did he do that to his coat? What did he say?"

Jess sniffed back the tears and explained as directly, simply, as he could. "When a Jew hears that someone has died, he says that. It means 'Blessed be the true judge.' And when a Jew mourns someone who has died, he tears a piece of his clothing."

"But who died, Jess, who?"

"I'm afraid . . ." he had to force the words out, "my father was mourning me. In his eyes, I have died."

Her hand flew to her mouth. "Oh, no . . ." she mumbled, "oh, Jesus . . ."

Jess was inconsolable, unreachable, for many hours. He sat on the sofa or paced the living room. Every once in a while she would touch his arm or take his hand or put her hand to his cheek. And he would say "I'm okay."

When she went to bed, he went out for a walk on the beach. She tried not to resent his father for so upsetting and saddening Jess. She knew from the look of the man's eyes as he ripped his coat that he himself was suffering pitifully, so it had not been intended as a cruel act. But the effect was cruel. Jess was cruelly hurt. And what hurt her, beyond having to see Jess suffer, was that his father's intrusion, however well meant, had closed Jess off from her. And more, it had

been her own intrusion on them, his father's seeing her
come into the room, that had seemed to trigger the
agony.

It was late in the night when she woke to hear the
piano—five slow, single notes being repeated over and
over. And then the melancholy voice of Jess—a plain-
tive voice thin and small like a child's—chanting with
the notes, "My name is Yussel . . ."

She wanted to go to him, hug him, talk to him.
Not only to ease his pain, but because there were
things on her mind too that she wanted to share with
him. But she knew that he didn't want her now, didn't
want anybody with him. And so she lay and listened to
the mournful chant, "My name is Yussel . . ."

In the morning, she let him sleep and left him a
note: "Doctor's appointment. See you at rehearsal.
Love you, Molly."

He read the note with dull eyes, holding it in limp
hands, sitting on the kitchen stool with drooping shoulders. He had been up most of the night, and though he
felt exhausted, his nerves were on edge. When he
poured the coffee, it splashed onto the counter. When
he took a sip, his hand shook and coffee dribbled down
his chin.

He needed to relax, but he didn't dare take one of
Molly's tranquilizers because it would knock him out,
the way he was feeling. He paced around, did some
stretching exercises, sat down at the piano, didn't like
the sound of the music. He got dressed, had another
cup of coffee, and waited for Bubba.

Bubba and one of the studio musicians would be
picking him up. He didn't want to talk to anybody. He
thought of calling a taxi and leaving a note on the door
for Bubba.

Finally that's what he did.

He arrived at Zany Gray's rehearsal hall before
any of the other musicians. Only technicians were
there, checking equipment, arranging microphones,
stringing wires. He didn't talk to anybody. He sat
down at the piano to run through "Love on the
Rocks." He didn't sing, just played the chords. He
didn't like the song the way it was, but he knew that

this particular morning he probably wouldn't like it any way at all. It would be better when they all put it together behind him and he sang. It was only a rehearsal. The music would lift him.

Some of the musicians drifted in, Jess nodded to them. Then came Bubba and the brothers and the piano player.

Bubba brought the piano player over. "Alan James, meet Jess Robin."

Jess nodded and yielded the piano.

Bubba nudged Jess aside. "What's up, my man?"

"Nothing, why?"

"You look like you're at a wake."

Jess smiled grimly at the irony. "Yeah, my own, right?"

"Somebody's. You ain't happy with the music?"

"Not particularly."

"Well, once we get rolling, it'll be fine."

"Yeah, let's get set up and get it done."

Technicians were still making final connections and adjustments when Jess called for a run-through of "Love on the Rocks." Just the instrumental parts—he wanted to listen.

He let them play without interruption, then muttered to himself, "Shit." He called to them, "Let's go through it again together."

He gave the downbeat, Bubba and the brothers played a short intro, then the orchestra came in, and then Jess:

"Love on the rocks ain't no surprise . . . Pour me a drink and I'll tell you some lies . . ."

Suddenly he stopped and wheeled on Bubba. "Hey, hold it!" The music trailed off and the musicians looked up. "Bubba, dammit! That's a minor note there. *Minor!*"

"Not on my sheet, it ain't." Bubba strummed the chord.

"Well, couldn't you *hear* it?"

"I heard it. I didn't think it sounded right. I was gonna ask you."

"When? Tomorrow? Don't ask, just open up your ears."

Bubba raised an eyebrow, then bent down to mark his sheet.

"Again, everybody, from the top."

They got nearly through the first verse when Jess stopped them again. "Too much cymbals back there. Sounds like a damn circus act! Again . . ."

This time they got through a couple of verses and the bridge. ". . . Hold it!"

Once more the musicians lowered their instruments and looked at him.

"Doesn't anybody here know about phrasing? The whole damn thing sounds mechanical, you're all just grinding it out. Play me some *music,* dammit! From the bridge again." He directed with his hand. ". . . two, three, four . . ."

They swung into it again.

Molly came quietly into the hall, smiling radiantly, and stood listening. She loved this song, sad and pessimistic as it was. It was one of those songs that could be a dirge sung by anybody else, but which Jess's timing and beat and strong voice made beautiful. Her smile vanished when Jess abruptly spun from the mike.

"Hold it, hold it!" He waved his arms angrily. "What's the matter with everybody? This music too difficult for you guys? There's nothing fancy here! Nobody's together, nobody's feeling anything, like some damn drum-and-bugle corps! We could put a laugh track to this and sell the whole damn thing to some damn variety show!"

He stomped back and forth in front of the musicians. "Tomorrow I'm taping my first TV shot and you guys are gonna make me look like a musical idiot—do you know that?"

The musicians looked at him stonily.

Jess snorted with disgust. "All right, this arrangements stinks anyway. Take five." They stood and stretched and milled around. Jess snatched up the charts and went over to the piano. "Alan, what the hell is this here?" He leaned down and traced a finger under a line. "It doesn't work."

Alan nodded and began fingering the piano, trying a slightly different riff.

Bubba went quickly over to Molly.

"What's the matter with everything?" she asked quietly. "What's going on? Something happen before I came?"

He waved her quiet. "Lay it on me, sister," he cocked his head, "what did the man say?"

"The world is minus one more rabbit."

"Hey, little momma!" He hugged her. "Congratulations! You feeling good? Everything good?"

"Everything's fine."

"Well, that is good news, hunh? The best kind of news. But, er-uh," he glanced at Jess, "I wouldn't tell him just right now."

"He's concentrating, hunh?"

"More like he's liable to punch you out."

"That bad? What happened?"

"Well, it's a long story. Seems like he's got a couple things on his mind. He don't seem like he wants to talk to nobody about it. But I don't know how much longer we can hack it, way it's going here."

"Okay," Jess interrupted, "come on, everybody. Let's get it right this time."

They took their places. Bubba ambled back toward the band.

Jess eyed him. "Speed it up, Bubba. I haven't got all day."

Bubba gave him a crooked smile and a hangdog look, shuffling his feet. "I'm movin' my black ass as fast as I can, massa Jess."

A few chuckles came from the band. Jess gritted his teeth and stared them into silence.

Jess stood at the mike. "Everybody ready?" Then he turned and added sardonically, "You sure?" He faced the mike. "All right, let's run it down again from the top . . . two, three, four . . ."

They got through the first eight bars without a noticeable hitch, but by now everybody was tight. Halfway through the second eight, Jess blew again.

"Dammit! The groove isn't there! It's not moving! Can't you *hear* it? There's no *flow* to it! It's worse than before!"

There were some mutterings from the band, a couple of muted sighs. Bubba fingered a few notes idly.

"You wanna play a solo or something, Bubba?"

"Nope." Bubba ceased his plucking. "Sorry."

"Something bugging you about this being *my* song played *my* way?"

Bubba just looked at him, saying nothing, showing nothing.

"You trying to show me up? You *want* me to look bad?"

"Hey, Jess, cool it," Bubba said softly.

"Cool it! You telling me to cool it?" Jess stalked over to him. "I'm the guy up front, remember?" Jess stood nose to nose with him, his jaw stuck out like a drill sergeant's. "I'm the guy that goes up or down with this gig, you forget that? I'm the guy everything's riding on. I wrote the music, I set it up, I gotta sing it. All you gotta do is get the backup right. If you can't get it right, you can take a walk."

Molly quickly wedged between them. "Stop it, Jess!"

"Stay out of this, Molly."

"This is crazy!"

"It's just between Bubba and me."

"Hell it is! It's just *you*. Boom, boom, boom! The only thing you haven't hollered for is more boom, boom, boom!"

Jess flinched. The allusion to the Keith Lennox incident jarred him. He looked away, feeling suddenly confused. Bubba looked down at his guitar.

Molly gestured toward the band. "You're not mad at them, Jess, you're mad at yourself."

"I just want the music right," he said lamely.

"No, that's not it. The music is fine. You've been out of your skull ever since your father came and—"

"I don't wanna hear about my father!" All eyes were on him, he felt ambushed and trapped.

Molly stuck her face into his just as he had done with Bubba before. "That's what it's all about, Jess. And you're laying it all on us because you can't handle it."

"Shut up, dammit!"

"And you won't even talk about it, you won't face it, because—"

"Shut up!" His arm was raised threateningly before he realized it. He saw Molly's stunned face, and Bubba's. He lowered his arm slowly and looked at his hand as if it were a strange, frightening weapon. He began backing away, shaking his head.

"Jess?"

He turned and started for the door, then broke into a run for it.

"Jess!"

He burst out the door and disappeared down the corridor. Bubba started after him, but Molly grabbed his arm.

"No, Bubba. Let him go. You can't do anything. He's got to work it out for himself."

"His father came?"

"It was a rough scene, Bubba."

"Maybe you better tell me about it."

"Okay. Can you straighten things out here, with the musicians and all? Then we'll take a walk."

"Done."

Jess didn't know where he was going, just out. He was frantic, as if being chased by a demon. He raced from the building and stood panting on the sidewalk. A cab pulled up to the curb, passengers got out. Jess shoved the last passenger aside and dove in.

"The airport!" He slammed the door.

Startled at first, the driver looked back at Jess, nodded, and eased the cab away from the curb.

"Fast!"

"Traffic's light. What time's your flight?"

"Now!"

The driver pushed down on the accelerator and moved into the fast lane. "What airline?"

"You pick it."

The driver glanced at him in the rearview mirror. "Where you going, friend?"

Jess sagged in the seat, feeling helpless and hopeless. "You can pick that too."

Jess was running. He had never run before, not away from anything. But he was sure as hell running away from something now—from everything. He knew he had cracked, but he wasn't crazy. Too much had happened too fast. He couldn't handle it anymore. Molly was right. "Just be cool," Bubba had advised him. Bubba was right too, but Jess couldn't be cool anymore. Maybe his father was right as well, that Jess was a deserter from everything, every place, to which he truly belonged.

Well, just right now it seemed that everybody was right except him. He couldn't stay, he couldn't go home. The only place he belonged now was no place.

He closed his eyes. He had no control over the forces that tore at him; no power over the memories, regrets, sadness, pain. All he could do was keep moving.

"... Maybe gentleness is out there somewhere, but it never has been anywhere for me ..."

Somewhere, anywhere, nowhere—all the same in the end, all nameless, endless, hopeless places where only dreams resided. "... Dreams may be eternity but let them speak just silently ..."

He kept his mouth shut just like his eyes and let his mind roll on, leaving him alone and empty, dazed and confused.

Chapter 9

Lines of a song kept going around in his head: "I sit alone beside the Dallas highway, breathing out my soul into the night . . . Travelin' on your own sure makes it easy, but runnin' from a wrong don't make it right."

That was as far as he got with it, putting it to a simple country melody. That was the thing about country-and-western music—it sang of simple things, everyday matters that people could identify with in their everyday lives. Barrooms, jukeboxes, lost loves, confessions, hitting the road—the stuff of country music. It surrounded him now, and he was drawn to it, part of it.

There wasn't much traffic on the highway this time of night. There wasn't much point in walking whatever endless miles remained between himself and the next Texas town, but he plodded along. The airline check might bounce, but that would be just another tough break for the airline. What money he had in his pocket was enough to buy a change of clothes, dungarees, and a small canvas athletic bag to put them in. And a cheap guitar. He had left everything behind but his music, and that was all in his head. The guitar was the first thing he bought. He had to have it for some reason. It was a companion. It was like holding on to his sanity.

Every once in a while a car whizzed by, or a truck, ignoring his thumb, the lights picking up the flat ribbon of asphalt. It was a long time before the red taillights disappeared.

Another set of lights, jiggling like they always did on a big rig. He turned around, backing up, and stuck out his thumb.

The truck slowed, came down in gear, and braked beside him. A shiny eighteen-wheeler with twin diesel stacks. He jumped up on the step, pulled open the door, and climbed in.

"You can throw your stuff in the sleeper back there," the driver said.

Jess put his guitar and bag on the bunk high behind the seat.

"Where you headin', friend?" The driver got it moving again, shifting smoothly up through the gears. He was lean, unshaven, wearing a cap that said CAT on the front.

"I'll know when I get there."

"You a singer?"

"Sometimes."

"We all are sometimes, ain't that a fact?"

"You're right. You are absolutely right."

"I dropped off a load in Albuquerque. Thought I'd head home for a few days."

"That sounds good."

"Home always sounds good, after you been driving for a couple weeks—ain't that the way with it?"

"Yeah, I guess it is."

Jess couldn't keep his eyes open. Now and then the driver said something, but it didn't seem to require an answer. He dozed fitfully, wakened occasionally by the rasping of the CB radio and the unintelligible lingo with which the driver responded.

When finally he blinked his eyes open to stay, it was early morning. Already the heat boiled up in shimmering waves above the road and across the dusty landscape. The driver was going through the gears. They were coming into a small town.

The driver looked over, saw Jess was awake, and nodded ahead. "Granville. My home town."

"Mine too."

"Oh, yeah?"

"Now."

"I got you." The driver chuckled. "I'll let you out wherever you want, otherwise I park my rig up ahead there, about a mile, pretty much right downtown, what there is of it."

"That'll be fine."

The driver eased the truck to the curb and shut it down, the diesel wheezing to a stop. "Here we are."

They both collected their things from the back and climbed down from their opposite doors.

"Thanks for the ride," Jess said.

"Don't mention it. Good luck."

Jess nodded. He watched the driver cross the street to a cluster of small houses. From one of them, a woman emerged, waiting. The driver trotted up to her and they embraced, then headed into the house, each with an arm around the other.

He turned away and headed back for a row of low buildings they had passed a few hundred yards before. He walked by a gas station, a hardware store, a shoe store, and stood in front of a bar with greasy windows over which a flickering sign said YELLOW ROSE. Peering through the windows, he could see a few tables, and a low platform with a microphone stand in the back.

He tried the door, it was open. The place smelled of beer, and some kind of pungent food—pizza or tacos, something like that. It was empty, except for a man behind the bar wiping it down with a soppy, gray towel. The man looked up as Jess came over. His gray hair was parted in the middle and slicked back. Around the biceps of his faded white shirt were black elastic bands.

"Good morning," Jess said.

"Morning." The man leaned on his hands.

"The boss around?"

"Lookin' at him. What can I do for you?"

"Well, unh, it looks like maybe you have music in here." Jess indicated the small platform in the rear.

"Now and again."

"Well, I'm looking for a job."

"What do you do?"

Jess held up his guitar. The man made no response. "I'm a guitar player."

"That a fact?"

"Well, I mean, I sing, and accompany myself on the guitar."

"That ain't news around here."

"No, I know, but—"

"Where you from?" The man's expression never changed, no smile, no frown.

"Well, I was living in L.A.—Los Angeles—but the life kind of got to me, you know? I was looking for a quiet place to—"

"Want a drink?"

"Okay."

"I don't hire nobody who drinks before breakfast."

Jess smiled wanly. "You got me there, mister. No, I don't want a drink. I need a job."

"Well, things ain't too busy right this minute, so I got a little extra time. Why don't you play me a song?"

"Unh . . ." Jess scratched his head. "I'm not at my best at eight o'clock in the morning."

"You a real mu-sician?"

"What do you want to hear?"

" 'You Are My Sunshine.' "

There was no hint of humor in the man's face. Jess didn't know if he was being put on or not. But he really had no choice. So, obligingly, he took out his guitar and sang: "You are my sunshine, my only sunshine . . ."

The man listened to two verses. Then he held up his hand and said, "You got the job, you start tonight. We got a group called Red Whooten and His Rednecks. Red took off a couple days ago. We keep it pretty simple for the folks come in here. Steady clientele, we give 'em what they want."

"Fine."

"You got a place to stay?"

"Not exactly."

"Rooming house, two blocks up. Miss Lilly's. Tell

her you're working at the Yellow Rose. Long as you're
here, you got a room."

"Thank you."

"Seven sharp."

The woman at the boardinghouse—Miss Lilly
herself, Jess assumed, though she didn't say—showed
him to a room in the back and, in a monotone, said,
"No noise, no liquor, no women." She handed him the
key and left him there.

He flopped down on the bed and closed his eyes.
Her words droned over and over again in his head, like
the line of a song, "No noise, no liquor, no women,"
until he fell asleep. He slept most of the day.

The Rednecks, three older fellows on guitar, ban-
jo, and drums, wore red shirts with black string ties.
The owner introduced Jess, and Jess said he'd pick up
a red shirt and string tie first chance he got.

The handful of tables were nearly filled up at
seven o'clock, and Jess surmised this was a town that
kept fairly early hours.

The band opened up with "Deep in the Heart of
Texas," with everybody in the bar singing along, and it
seemed that it was perhaps their theme song. Then
they went into a series of what were apparently old
standards—Jess recognized some of the melodies, but
the melodies resembled one another anyway. He faked
it where he didn't know, strumming chords once he
had the key, and coming in to sing the choruses the
second time around. He did happen to know "South of
the Border" and some of "Goodbye, Little Darlin',
Goodbye" well enough to take the lead.

After tonight's gig, he would sit down with the
boys and copy some of the words to their other favorites. Tonight he would just get through it.

They played for about an hour, then the other
guitarist, whose name was Gaylord, called, "Break."

Jess announced into the mike, "Okay, folks,
thank you very much. Don't go away now, we'll just
take a ten-minute break and then we'll be right back
with more of your favorites."

Before he could turn away, a young woman at the

front table, whose companion had kept his arm around her the entire hour, waved eagerly.

"Oh, please, could you sing 'Luckenbach, Texas?' "

The rest of the band was already off, gone into the back room where they would be set up with drinks and where they could relax. Jess had never heard of the song.

"We're just going on a ten-minute break, ma'am," Jess drawled as best he could, "and then we'll be right back and sing it for you."

"I just want a solo, like Johnny Cash. Please," she folded her hands prayerfully, "it's my birthday."

"Just ten minutes."

"Hey, hold on there!" her escort said, standing up. He was a fairly big man. "You want a song, honey, by God you're gonna get one." The man tossed down his latest shot and walked up to Jess. "Listen, mudsucker, you're paid to entertain, not take breaks. And my lady wants to be entertained."

"I ain't paid by you, mister."

"I don't take no lip." The man stepped onto the platform.

Jess poked him in the stomach with the end of the guitar, and the man stumbled backward off the stage and plopped down into his lady's lap.

Chairs squeaked and banged as other men got up. The owner rushed around from behind the bar and stood between Jess and the patrons, facing them and holding up his hands. "Okay, okay, everybody just cool on down." He called to the back, "Gaylord, get in here!"

Then he faced Jess, his hands on his hips. "You sing real nice, mister, but you got a bad attitude. These folks here is *friends,* and we entertain all special requests."

Then he bent down to the girl, who was still hosting her escort in her lap. "What was the name of that song you wanted to hear?"

" 'Luckenbach, Texas,' " she said, helping her man off her.

Jess edged off to the side. Gaylord positioned himself in front of the mike, smiling at the woman. "Happy birthday, honey."

Gaylord strummed the intro, the owner glared at Jess and hooked a thumb unmistakably in the direction of the front door.

Jess packed up his guitar and walked out.

Whatever kind of communication network they had in this town, it was fast. By the time Jess reached the rooming house, his bag was already outside the door, his few clothes jammed into it.

Another trucker, another town, another bar, this one called The Happy Pinto. No band there, just himself and his guitar. A small group of drinkers, hats shoved back on their heads, arms around their women, guffawing, slurping their Pearl beer.

"Well, folks," Jess announced without benefit of a mike, "I'm new here, but I'll try and—"

"Then start off with 'Rodeo Cowboy!'" somebody called.

Jess cleared his throat and strummed idly. "Well, I don't know that one too well, so maybe—"

"Who the hell don't know 'Rodeo Cowboy'" came another voice from the bar.

Jess started to sing "South of the Border," which had been acceptable at the last place, and which he remembered for some reason from childhood.

Hoots came from the patrons.

"That's a hunnert years old!" somebody yelled.

"And he ain't no Gene Autry neither!" came from somebody else.

"Bobby Joe, get up there'n sing 'Rodeo Cowboy.'"

It was probably Bobby Joe who slid his chair back and headed for Jess's place. The manager or owner, whoever it was that had hired Jess, was nowhere to be seen.

"Get offa there, boy, and let a singer sing!"

Jess packed up his guitar once again and walked out.

Jess would have nothing more to do with music. He was empty, too lonely to sit still in one place. He wandered, taking odd jobs wherever he could find them.

He got rides from an assortment of people whose variety surprised him. A suave black businessman in a Lincoln Continental picked him up, lectured him on what made this country great, and let him out a few miles further on the same small highway.

A rancher stopped his dilapidated pickup truck to let Jess in.

"You want work?" the man asked, his tattered ten-gallon hat pulled down over his leathery face, hiding his eyes.

"Yup."

"You know fences?"

"I can learn."

For a few days he was put to work wearing rawhide gloves to repair barbed-wire fences around the man's spread. He ate in the man's house, served by the man's silent, fat wife. At the end of two weeks, his stomach couldn't take the food anymore. He was paid $20 and sent on his way.

A crew of oil-rig workers riding the flatbed of a truck hauled him aboard and said there was always some work around the cookhouse or cleaning gear. He worked at the small, low-yield oil field for a couple of months until a fight broke out among the workers and bosses over late paychecks, and the foreman fired them all.

An Indian who bred quarterhorses offered him a job mucking out stalls. The horses scared him, but he hung in for a while until a stallion he was trying to work around kicked him in the thigh and bit him in the shoulder.

He got a job in a roadside diner helping the Chinese cook. The heat and stench of the cooking made him dizzy. The Chinaman never complained, never said a word in fact. One day when Jess was pounding out some flat patties of dough, he watched the Chinaman leaning over a steaming pot of stew, stirring it with a wooden spoon. The man's sweat dripped an endless stream into the pot. Jess couldn't take it anymore. Holding his stomach, he quickly left through the back door.

He continued to wander, picking fruit and vegetables, painting houses and barns, mopping floors in restaurants—taking virtually anything that was offered, not staying long anyplace. He sold his guitar for $25, and continued to have nothing to do with music.

Two swarthy men Jess supposed were Mexicans, since they spoke in Spanish accents, offered him a ride in their Camaro. He sat in the back. Between the two front seats was a spittoon, which the men used often.

"Where you going?" the driver asked.

"Nowhere special."

The two men looked at each other.

"You need money?"

"Yeah."

They looked at each other again and didn't speak for a while.

Then the man opposite the driver turned around and scrutinized Jess. His eyes were small, narrowed by his look. His teeth were crooked. A scar caused one eye to droop. Another scar curled his lip into half a smile.

"We could use a guy," the man said.

"I can do just about anything."

"Special kind of guy."

"How special?"

"Kind of guy can be trusted."

"I can be trusted."

The man faced front again, and he and the driver mumbled in Spanish.

Then the man turned back to Jess. "We meeting a plane tonight. In a field. We unload the plane. You can be the lookout."

Jess studied the man. "What's on the plane?"

"Not your business."

"I don't know."

"You need money?"

"Yeah, but I don't know about this."

"We already decide, you be the lookout."

"I think I'll pass on that."

The man blinked slowly, and the scar twitched around his lip. "No, you not pass now. We already tell you."

"I think you can drop me off right here."

"Not drop you off either. Now you work with us."

Jess let a few seconds pass. Then he lunged over the seat, whacking the man away with his right elbow and grabbing the wheel with his left hand, yanking it around. The car careened, the driver hit the brakes, the car skidded off the road, back on, spun the other way.

While the driver wrestled for control and the car slowed, Jess tumbled into the front seat, at the same time slamming a fist into the other man's belly. He pulled the door handle, heaved his shoulder against the door, and rolled out.

He was lucky it was the shoulder of the road and not the pavement. He rolled over and over until he hit the patch of tall grass. Then he scrambled to his feet and ran.

He did not look back right away, and when he did, he could see that they were not chasing him. Over a rise, he could see the dust cloud fanning out and wafting away from where the car had spun. The car was hidden by the hill.

He kept moving away, now at a trot. His shirt and pants were torn, and some blood trickled down his arm and leg, but he had only been scraped up, he was not hurt.

Suddenly, the idea of making music in a bar, even if it was not his own music, didn't seem half bad.

He followed some fences to a farmhouse. He snatched some dungarees off a clothesline and slipped away into a thicket of slender trees and brambles. He cleaned himself off in a stream and put on the nearly dry clothes. They were a little large, but manageable.

He walked along a dirt road for a couple of hours until he came to a small town—how many small towns had he seen in recent months? All he needed to find was a bar with a piano.

He was quickly hired, for meals not money, at a place called Mac's Lone Star, which served hot and cold sandwiches and chicken fried steak. He didn't play regular sets, but background music for the boisterous eating and backslapping. Occasionally somebody listened, somebody requested something, but nobody pressured him.

He noodled around with different kinds of songs before falling into the gentle strains of "God Didn't Make Little Green Apples."

And for the first time in months, he sang.

"If that's not lovin' me, then all I've got to say: God didn't make little green apples and it don't rain in Indianapolis in the summertime . . ."

It felt good to sing, even better to hear the surprising applause. He was asked to sing it again, and did.

"No such thing as Doctor Seuss, Disneyland and Mother Goose is no nursery rhyme . . ."

At the end of the evening, a portly man in a beige suit, white boots, and a white Stetson came over to the piano.

"Well now," the man said, fingering his string tie that was held together by a turquoise eagle, "I consider it fortunate that I stopped by this evenin'. I'm Johnny Mac himself, and I like your music, son."

"Thank you," Jess said, hungry and anxious to get his supper before they closed down the kitchen.

"My name don't mean nothing to you?"

"I'm sorry, I don't think so."

"I own this place, and a couple of others. And I like to give young musicians a chance, take pride in it. Now, this here place . . ." he waved around at the emptying tables, "this is fine, but I'd like to spread your music around some. How you feel about that?"

"Well, unh, that's fine. What do you mean?"

"I got a bar over in Mercy, kind of a down-home place, quiet. I'd like to try you over there. Then my biggest place is in Fort Worth. Place called Mac's Royale. What's your name, son?"

"Jess Robin."

"Jess Robin. Why is that name familiar?"

"Couldn't tell you."

"Well, Mr. Jess Robin, I'd like to move you around a bit, give you some billing—you know, signs in the windows we can have drawn up, announcements of upcoming stars, that kind of thing. How you feel about that?"

"Actually, I'm not much for publicity, Mr., unh, Mac. I like to kind of keep it low-key."

"Nonsense, son. You got talent. I can spot it. You ain't exactly country, you ain't exactly western. What are you, exactly?"

"Jewish," Jess surprised himself by saying.

"Haw, haw." Johnny Mac slapped Jess on the back. "Well, son, if that's a joke, don't tell it too often around hyere. And if it's true, don't tell it never. Look," he bent down to whisper, "we'll give it a couple more nights here, okay? And I'll put up a sign in my place over in Mercy announcing you're coming in. See how it goes there. Then maybe Fort Worth, hunh? We'll give you some time to get known."

"What if I'd rather just stay here?"

"No deal." Mac straightened up. "I keep people moving. I ain't gonna make no money on you here."

"You aren't spending any either."

Mac frowned, then smiled, then laughed and squeezed the back of Jess's neck. "I appreciate that, I really do. Yes sir, like we say around hyere, two things we really appreciate: a little sass, a little music, a lot of women."

"That's three."

"So drop the sass. You got a chance with me, son. And I figure you like to play. Over in Mercy you make a salary. I figure you ain't got much to lose."

"You're right there."

"Well, I ain't been wrong yet, have I?"

The place in Mercy, called Mac's Mixer, was no larger than the first place, maybe smaller. It was quiet, like Mac said, mainly somber drinkers.

Jess played simple stuff, sang once in a while, incorporating a few obscure country ballads the words to which he had picked up in his travels. A few people screwed their heads around at the bar to watch him, otherwise he was paid little heed.

Toward the end of the first night, only the bartender and a woman were left. She looked to be in her fifties, with bleached hair done up in a beehive, heavy makeup on her face, a skin tight black dress that showed folds of flesh, black mesh stockings, and mile-high stiletto heels. She had been there on and off through the evening; Jess had seen her leave a couple of times with a couple of different men.

Jess sang "Little Green Apples," just because he liked the feel of it ". . . And if that's not loving me, then all I've got to say . . ."

The bartender and the woman applauded. The bartender was mopping up. He called over, "Okay, Jess, let's knock it off. Time to go home."

The woman wrinkled up her nose and flapped her hand. "Aw . . ." She smiled at Jess.

Jess smiled back. "Don't you want to go home?"

"Not particularly. Nothing to go home to, nobody." She caught the bartender's hand as he was passing by. "Couldn't he play one more song, Freddy, hunh?"

The bartender shrugged, leaving it to Jess.

"What kind of song would you like?" Jess asked, rolling over a few chords with his hands.

She put a hand to her cheek and looked up thoughtfully. "Play me a sad song. Maybe it'll make me happy."

Jess fiddled around with some notes. It had been so many months since he'd played anything of his own. Somehow he felt like it now. And there was just the three of them. "Okay," he said at last, "I hope it makes you happy."

He set up the opening chords of "Love on the Rocks," and sang:

"Love on the rocks ain't no surprise . . . Pour me a drink and I'll tell you some lies . . . Yesterday's gone and now all I want is a smile . . ."

He smiled over at her, but she didn't smile back, just nodded to the beat.

"Got nothin' to lose . . . So you just sing the blues all the time . . . Gave you my heart . . . Gave you my soul . . . You left me alone here . . . With nothing to hold."

She clasped her hands under her chin. The bartender leaned on his elbows to listen.

". . . Love on the rocks ain't no surprise . . . Pour me a drink and I'll tell you some lies . . . Yesterday's gone and now all I want is a smile . . ."

When he finished, there were tears on her cheeks, but she was smiling.

"Thank you," she said, "thank you very much. I loved that song when it came out. You sound a lot like the guy on the record." She left the barstool and came over. She glanced back at the bartender, who was busy counting money from the register, and said softly, "I don't suppose you'd like to come with—"

"No, no thanks. I hope that song was okay for you."

"It was beautiful. Just what I wanted. It must be wonderful to make music like that. You're so lucky."

Jess looked at her eyes, old beyond their time, sad even when she smiled. "Yeah, I am. I'm glad you enjoyed it."

"Will you be playing tomorrow night?"

"Be right here."

"Play that again, just for me, tomorrow night?"

"You got it."

But he wasn't there the next night. Johnny Mac picked him up.

'Got a spot for you at Mac's Royale," Mac said as Jess put his bag in the trunk. Mac slammed the lid. "Lucky an opening came up. I already got people talking about you over there."

Mac's Royale, on the outskirts of Fort Worth, did indeed have a cardboard sign propped up in the window: TONIGHT—FEATURING—JESS ROBIN!! In smaller letters, it said: DIRECT FROM CHICAGO.

"Chicago?" Jess said as he trailed Mac into the place.

"Saves a lot of questions. You don't sound Texas.

Part of the buildup. I even put a little ad in the paper. Fort Worth, kid, the big time."

The place was but a minor step up from the first two—a little larger, a little cleaner, the piano tuned a little better. But it was still no more than a dusty bar. Jess was clearly going nowhere with Mac's series of night spots. He was tired of the piano, wanted his guitar, wanted out of bars.

He played listlessly. A little applause occasionally greeted the end of a song. Mac told him he had a week here solid. Jess would not last a week. Maybe he'd get out of this part of the country entirely, maybe try Florida. At least there wasn't so much dust in Florida.

He found himself thinking of the woman at the last place, the woman who really liked his music, who thought he was so lucky to be able to "make music like that." And he was lucky. Except that his idea of making music was not to make it for himself, but to make it for others, to give them pleasure, to be appreciated.

He wanted an audience. These people here, in this bar, were not an audience. They were here to drink and laugh and talk, and only occasionally to listen. He couldn't play for that anymore. He would stick it out for another couple of days, until Johnny Mac came up with his first paycheck.

He was vamping on the piano between songs, and drifted into some minor chords. He had half a notion to come up with *"Hava Nagillah,"* just to see what would happen. His eyes roamed the smoky bar, then came back to the keyboard.

His head snapped up. Somebody had just turned from the bar toward the piano with a couple of beers. And at first Jess hadn't even noticed. Then it struck him. He squinted at the man through the haze. The large, smiling black man headed for him.

"Bubba!" he cried, leaping up, causing all the heads to swivel around. "Bubba!" He slung himself around the piano and threw his arms around his friend.

"Hey, hey, hold it, my man. You spilling the beer."

᎙ᵘᵉ "Bubba, dammit, how the hell are you? How did you find me?"

"One musician can always find another. Things sound like they're draggin' a little in here, thought maybe you could come up with a number that had a little more boom, boom, boom."

Jess leaned back against the piano, stunned, overjoyed, full of wonder at the magical appearance of his friend.

Bubba put the beers down on the piano and gave Jess a hug. "Wasn't all that easy, though," Bubba said, patting his back. "Lost the trail a couple of times. Friend down here, he happened to see these little signs popping up here and there with your name on 'em. And then he saw this ad someplace. You must have some stories to tell by now."

"A couple, Bubba, a couple. Hey, let me look at you." He held Bubba off by the biceps. "Damn, what a sight to see."

"Yeah." Bubba glanced around. "Speaking of sights, I think this crowd is tired of this one. Maybe you better play something."

"In a minute. Okay, Bubba," Jess suddenly dropped his smile, "lay it on me. Tell me why you're here. It's not just to find me. It's either Papa ... or Molly."

"None of the above, my man. It's a whole brand-new person called Charlie Parker Rabinovitch."

"Charlie Par ..." Recognition spread slowly over his face like dawn. "You can't mean ..."

"That's right, my man. After Molly's two favorite musicians. Eight pounds, ten ounces, and he wails like a cantor with saxophone pipes."

"Holy ..." Jess covered his eyes. He kept moving his mouth but couldn't say anything.

"Well, that's all *my* news," Bubba said with exaggerated casualness. He took a drink of beer.

"Well ... well ..." Jess stammered. "Let's get outta here!"

"After you, my man." Bubba gestured grandly, with a bow. "Car's at the curb, plane's at the gate. Flight leaves in an hour."

Jess started away, Bubba grabbed his arm and hauled him back, grinning. "By the way, he don't *look* like Charlie Parker . . ."

Jess ripped his arm free and zigzagged among the tables headed for the door, Bubba one step behind.

Chapter 10

Jess wanted to surprise Molly with his return, but Bubba said he didn't think that was quite fair.

"You already surprised her when you left, my man," he said, "and just when she was gonna surprise you with the news. She's got a right to be ready for you when you come back."

"Yeah, I guess you're right."

Bubba had brought him a packet of mail—not all of it, he said, but the stuff that seemed important—and Jess leafed through it on the plane. He immediately opened a couple of letters and read them carefully.

"I'm going to marry her, Bubba."

"Well, that's a very nice idea. She gonna marry you?"

Jess paused and looked up. "Why not? Something you're not telling me?"

"Nope. Just it's usually a two-way street. Last I knew you were already blocked on one way."

"Already married, you mean."

"Something like that."

"Rivka filed for a divorce, before I left L.A. I signed the papers." Jess fluttered the two letters in his hand. "And there's a guy she wants to marry."

"How you feel about that?"

"It's right. I'm happy for her."

"So that just leaves Molly."

"She'll marry me. Won't she? She still loves me, doesn't she, Bubba?"

"We never talked about that. It's been a long time."

"There's not ... I mean, she doesn't have ... there isn't anybody—"

"Not that I know of. But Molly, she's been getting along pretty good on her own. You may have to convince her you plan to stay around a year or two."

"I'm done running. She'll know."

Bubba grinned. "Yeah, she probably will."

"She loves me, you know she does. You must have talked about it."

Bubba smiled slyly. "You know how I feel about that kind of talk."

"She loves me," Jess said, satisfied.

Any doubt that might have remained was instantly erased when Molly opened the door and hurled herself into a hug with him, kissing his shoulder, his neck, his cheek, his lips.

Tears rolled down both their cheeks.

"I don't deserve you, Molly." He rocked her as they hugged and kissed.

"Just make an honest woman out of me."

"Then you'll marry me? You'll marry me?"

"It's a distinct possibility. I've always wanted to marry a singer with a gold record."

"It went gold? My song?" He leaned back to look at her.

"Your album. Surely you knew ..."

"Couple people mentioned something here and there, about my songs being familiar."

"You sure been out of touch."

"I want to tell you everything."

"There's plenty of time, right?"

"Yeah. Let me see him."

Charlie Parker Rabinovitch was a bubbly, gurgly, tiny, and active baby, arms and legs wiggling like an overturned beetle.

She started to pick him up out of the crib.

"No," Jess stopped her, "just let me look at him for a minute."

"He's got all his fingers and toes, everything's in place."

"Yeah." Jess was dazzled by the sight, the little figure, pale pink, wearing a little blue top, white diapers with a shiny outer layer, lying in white sheets. "He doesn't look like anybody."

"Like you, silly," she put an arm around him, "he looks like you. He's going to have a nice cleft chin, just like yours."

"His hair isn't very dark."

"It'll get darker. Come on," she leaned over the crib to take him, "you can't put it off. You've got to hold him. You better get used to it."

Jess clutched his son, afraid to hold him too tightly but wanting to feel him. Warm bubbles from the baby's mouth soaked into his shirt. "He's beautiful."

"Yes, he is."

"Like you."

"Thank you."

"I can't believe he's mine."

"Well, you missed some of the important times."

"I can't tell you how sorry I—"

"Don't worry, I'll fill you in. He's yours, all right. And don't forget it."

"I love you, Molly."

"I love you too, schmuck."

Wedded bliss. The term had been only a meaningless, trite expression before, but he learned that, as with most things trite, there was a basis in truth. He was experiencing wedded bliss. The City Hall ceremony had been perfectly simple.

And fatherhood bliss. Jess suddenly felt that he had an unshakable purpose to his life. He carried a snapshot of Charlie Parker Rabinovitch in his wallet.

The purpose was not simple. It involved not only being a father and husband (that position of the terms, reversed from usual order, asserted itself in his mind because it too was the truth; he was a father first), but also his music. Being away from his own music for so long had reinforced its importance to him. He returned at once to his guitar and his songs, and worked with Bubba and the brothers to sharpen them.

His guitar nestled under his arm as comfortably as if he had never been separated from it. The tips of his fingers toughened quickly. And while his fingering of the strings was a little clumsy at first, it presented no more difficulty than a tennis player's getting the groove back in his serve after a few weeks' layoff.

Sooner than he had expected, and surely helped by his general sense of peace and confidence, he was playing better than ever. His voice had never left him much, and he was feeling his music as never before.

In short, he was ready to go.

"Well," Molly said, "how do you want to play it?"

"I want Zany Gray," Jess said in the manner of a challenger calling for a title shot in the ring. "I flaked out on him last time, I want another try."

"That'll be tough, Jess. You didn't leave the clown too happy last time out."

"You saying you can't pull it off?" he taunted her.

"Did you hear me say that? I didn't hear me say that. All I heard was, that'll be tough."

"So?"

"So, let's sign another contract and I'll get to work."

They gave each other a hug and a kiss. Several, in fact. In fact, they made love.

"Now that's what I call a long-term contract," Molly said, stretching out languidly beside him.

Eddie Gibbs came out of his office and strolled across the parking lot, admiring with every step his beautiful new white Rolls Royce. He stopped a few yards away from it, drinking it in. What greater mark of a man's success could there be than a new Rolls in a parking spot where there was a little wooden sign bearing his very own name?

He spread his arms toward it as if to say, "There you have it, folks, isn't it everything I promised it would be?"

He slid into the plush seat and settled into his luxurious cocoon, enjoying the pride and power of ownership for a few seconds before he started the engine.

Suddenly the passenger door lurched open and Molly slid in. "Pretend you don't know me."

Eddie closed his eyes. "Don't tell me."

"You don't know me?"

"Mr. Wonderful is back."

"Yup."

"Don't tell me."

"I didn't."

"But here you are."

"Yup."

"And you're going to tell me something."

"He's back just in time for Zany Gray's autumn special from New York."

"Are you kidding?"

"Am I laughing?"

He slapped the steering wheel, then caressed it as if in apology. "He walked out on Zany last year. You know what grief that caused me?"

"I know Zany's TV show went on without a hitch, just as if nothing had happened. And Zany's career hasn't missed a beat."

"But the *grief* I went through."

"Hey, we all go through grief. The point is, the client didn't suffer—isn't that the point? Isn't that our job?"

"The answer is no."

"You haven't heard the question."

"Ask."

"One song. That's all I'm asking."

"No!"

"Dammit, you owe him!"

"What do I owe? He took a hike—"

"His album went gold."

"A year ago. Who remembers a year ago?"

"I'll bet your commission paid for this car."

Eddie sighed.

"You don't see me wearing furs, do you? You got it all. So you owe me too."

Eddie shook his head. He backed the car up and turned out of the lot. "Where can I drop you?"

"New York."

"Forget it."

"You owe him!"

"I hate him!"

"I love him!" She lowered her voice. "And anyway, you wouldn't want to find this beautiful hunk of machinery all dented up one morning, would you?"

"You wouldn't do that."

"I might go crazy."

"You *are* crazy!"

"So are you, if you don't know that Jess Robin is about to go sky high, through the roof! And he'll give Zany's special the zing it needs! And you get a piece of all that, unless you're crazy!"

"Enough! Okay!" He gripped the steering wheel hard, knuckles going white, face red. "One number!" He held up a quivering finger. "One! At scale! Not one cent more! One song . . . two-and-a-half minutes!"

"Three!"

"Two-and-a-half!"

"Three-and-a-half!"

"Three! All right, Molly, three is all you get."

She leaned over and kissed him on the cheek. "You're such a nice man. Thank you, Eddie."

September in New York was hot, as warm as Los Angeles and more humid. The leaves in Central Park were turning a dingy brown as if in losing their lives they were taking on the tones of the surrounding buildings.

Further downtown on the West Side, the marquee outside the TV studio announced: ZANY GRAY'S AUTUMN IN NEW YORK—THURSDAY NIGHT.

It was Tuesday, and in one of the studio rooms, Jess and the orchestra had finished running through Jess's new song, "America," and now they were listening intently to a playback of the tape. Molly and Eddie

Gibbs sat off to the side, listening, watching Jess for reactions.

Jess listened with head bowed, hand covering his face, concentrating. When it was finished, he thought for a moment, then looked over at Molly. "What do you think?"

"It's fantastic, Jess!" Eddie put in.

Jess ignored him. "Molly?"

"Next time around, I'd like to hear a little more piano."

"Mmm." Jess asked to hear the final few bars again, heard them, then nodded. "You're right." He turned to one of the technicians, who was sitting with his earphones slung around his neck. "How about that, Jimmy? Can we do it again, but with more piano this time?"

Jimmy glanced at his watch. "Sorry, Jess, but it'll have to wait for Thursday's rehearsal."

Eddie jumped up. "What's wrong with tomorrow? This is important. Why do we have to wait?"

"Jewish holiday, Eddie, Yom Kippur." Jess waved around at the musicians and crew. "Some of you guys had better take off if you're going to make shul by sundown."

Some of them waved and quickly left.

Eddie sighed. "Day of Atonement."

"You got it right."

"Couldn't come at a worse time."

"Don't worry, it'll be all right. We're close. Another couple times through, we got it."

"Don't get me wrong, I'm not opposed to the holiday."

Jess walked over and gave him a friendly pat on the head. "Wouldn't matter if you were, would it?"

"Mr. Robin?"

Jess saw a studio page escorting his Uncle Leo toward him. "Leo!"

"Yussel."

They hugged each other briefly.

"What are you doing here, Leo? Didn't you get the tickets for the show?"

"The tickets I got. It's not the tickets, Yussel."

"Well?"

"Well, well, well . . ." Leo gestured rhythmically with his palms up, like the Pope welcoming a crowd at the Vatican.

"Okay, I know." Jess shifted uncomfortably. "Forget it, Leo. If you've come to get me together with Papa, forget it. It won't work. There's nothing you can do."

"Listen to me, Yussel," Leo waggled a finger at him, "this is different. He's got high blood pressure, your father—"

"He's sick?"

"Give me a minute. It's not serious, but he just has to take it easy. The doctor won't let him sing tonight." He paused. "Yussel, you know what this means? The first time in five generations a Rabinovitch won't be singing '*Kol Nidre*' on Yom Kippur!"

Jess turned away, sighed, then turned back. "Did Papa put you up to this?"

"No, no," Leo shook his head briskly, "he said nothing to me. The doctor told me the blood pressure and the order. The rest is just me talking. Just me personally." He lowered his eyes and pursed his lips. "I was just thinking that tonight, since you're right here in New York, maybe you could sing '*Kol Nidre*' in his place."

"No way, Leo."

"What it would mean to—"

"I can't. That's all there is to it. I just can't."

Leo hung his head.

Molly put her hand on Jess's shoulder. "Why not, Jess? I think you should do it. I think you have to."

"Why? He won't take my calls, he won't answer my letters, he won't have anything to do with me."

"Well . . . well . . ." Leo said hesitantly, "it's not just your father I was thinking about."

"Sorry, Leo. I'll see you Thursday." Jess tapped his uncle on the arm, paused a moment to smile, then walked away to the piano, where he started collecting his sheet music.

Leo shrugged at Molly. Molly shrugged back and watched him leave.

Then she came casually over to Jess, picked up a sheet he had dropped, and handed it to him. "I don't understand your point, you know."

"What point? My father made his own decision about me. It wasn't my idea. There's nothing I can do about it."

"You're being as stubborn as he is."

"Stubborn! This isn't a matter of stubborn. He wrote me off, Molly!"

"Did you write him off?"

"Don't start, Molly!" He turned to the side and held his hand up to her, like stopping traffic. "I'm dead to him, case closed!"

She pushed his hand away. "Case reopened. There's no reason we can't talk about it."

"I won't go crawling to my father!" His back was to her, and he clenched and unclenched his hands at his sides.

"Not stubborn, hunh? You call it crawling? So you won't crawl. Well, I'm not asking you to crawl, just to consider. Consider us. Because I think there's something you don't realize, something I can never forget. It was me who walked in on you two when you were talking in our apartment. And what were you talking about? Singing? I don't think so, Jess. Because it was me your father was looking at when he tore the lapel off his coat. Me, Jess. So what was the final straw between you? You want me to tell you?"

"No."

"Me. And do you know what that means? That means, unless you try to reach him—I mean really try, not call, not write, but do something that really means something, like singing tonight—unless you try, this whole thing will always be in our way. It will always stand between us."

"I don't want to talk about it anymore."

"Neither do I." She walked briskly out of the room.

It was not like Molly, and he was stunned. It was not like her to walk out, not like her to want to end a discussion of a disagreement between them. It was her way to persist—not for the sake of argument, but to talk it out, to come to a point of agreement even if it was to agree to disagree.

So he was quite profoundly unsettled. Her abrupt and discomforting withdrawal made him think about what he didn't want to think about. He had not been aware of her sense of inclusion in this matter of father and son. Nor was he aware that he was being stubborn. He had thought of it simply as his acceptance of rejection by his father. But now he had himself rejected Leo and even Molly.

And by implication he had rejected his father. Rejection of people one loves is a form of running away, evasion. And Lord knows, he had had enough of running away.

A full congregation in the small synagogue rose, prayer books in hand and eyes glued to them, for the singing of the *"Kol Nidre."* In an unaccustomed place in the third row stood Cantor Rabinovitch, in a blue suit over which he wore his tallith. He did not hold a prayer book, for he knew the text well. Nor were his eyes open. He stood mouthing the words as the voice of a substitute cantor, backed by a small male choir, sang from the pulpit.

The cantor was Mr. Frankel, a small man with a voice that sounded small in comparison with that to which the congregation was usually treated. But he sang dutifully, precisely.

When Jess came onto the dais in his robes, Cantor Frankel saw him and recognized the situation immediately, nodded, and moved aside. Jess smoothly took over the singing, and his voice rose above the others, lifting the *"Kol Nidre"* chant to its full, rich glory.

At the sound of the voice, Cantor Rabinovitch's eyes popped open to see Jess, in front of the choir, now leading the congregation in the final repetition of this holiest of prayers.

Jess met his father's shocked gaze with his own calm and confident eyes, and felt his voice fill even more, gain strength. Jess felt a sense of reverent triumph and satisfaction, even as his father again shut his eyes.

At the conclusion, Jess left the stage hurriedly, aware that the congregation was abuzz over the surprise performance they had seen and heard.

In the social hall, the only illumination came from the yahrzeit candles. The door swung open, Cantor Rabinovitch trudged in, took his coat from the closet, wearily pulled it on, and started across the hall toward the exit.

Jess cleared his throat noisily so as not to surprise his father unduly—before he stepped out from the shadows near the wall. He gently took his father's arm. "Papa, we have to talk."

Through the thick glasses, the old man's eyes never changed. He looked down at the hand on his arm. "Young man," he said coldly, "you will please remove your hand." He resumed his slow pace toward the door.

Even with what had gone before, and with his now having sung the *"Kol Nidre,"* Jess was not prepared for this reaction, so distant and detached. He hesitated a moment before quickly catching up to his father and turning in front of him, blocking his way. "It's been over a year, Papa. Isn't that long enough?"

"Please let me pass."

"No, not yet. We can face each other, we must, Papa. It's *Kol Nidre,* it's Yom Kippur, a day for forgiveness."

"A day to atone for your sins," the cantor added stiffly.

"What sins, Papa?"

"For each to decide in his own way. Please let me pass."

"But is it a sin to serve God in my own way, Papa?"

"Let God Himself judge."

"Yes, Papa, let Him judge. Don't judge me so harshly yourself. If I don't feel called to be a cantor, so let God judge. If I want to write music, sing my own songs, let Him judge that too. Is it really being sinful, what I want to do? With God as my judge, Papa, I don't think it is sinful. It is not wrong."

"May I go now?"

"Please, Papa, listen to me." Jess started to put his hands on his father's arm, but drew back. "You used to say, 'You have to know where you came from before you know where you're going.' Well, I know where I came from and I know where I'm going. I have my own congregation now and, you know, Papa, they say they love my music. It gives them pleasure, gives them enjoyment. Is that a sin, Papa, to bring enjoyment to people?"

The cantor closed his eyes. "I know nothing of such other congregations, especially what you call your own. I know only of the one which I serve. I am too tired for your questions . . ."

"And my wife." Jess thought his father flinched at the mention. "Yes, my wife, Molly. To marry a woman that you love deeply, is that a sin? Is that something for which one asks forgiveness, or makes atonement?"

"You test my wisdom. I'm afraid I'm not so wise. I know of one wife, now I am asked about a second. I cannot make these judgments for you."

"But you *have* made them, Papa, haven't you? And you have made them hard, hard enough to cause me pain, and perhaps yourself. If I *have* committed sins, Papa, in your eyes, then I deserve to know what they are, to hear it from you. How else can I atone?"

The old man kept his eyes closed, and rocked slightly from side to side.

Jess dug out his wallet and slid from its pouch the snapshot. He lifted his father's hand and lay the photograph in the palm. "Look, Papa. It's your grandson. Named after two great musicians. His name is Chaim Parker Rabinovitch."

His father slowly opened his eyes and mouthed silently, "Rabinovitch."

"Yes, Papa, Rabinovitch. Not Robin. My wife's name, and my son's—like mine, like yours—is Rabinovitch. The sixth generation. Look closely, Papa, and see if he doesn't have Mama's eyes."

Slowly, almost painfully, the old man lowered his eyes until they rested on the photograph in the palm of his hand.

"Tonight, Papa, I was a cantor again. Perhaps a part of me will always be a cantor. Because I am a part of you. And so is he. Unless ... unless ... I am not your son, and then he is not your grandson. If that is a judgment you can make, so be it. But it is not a judgment I can make. I don't know so much about the old ways, but I know this: I will never tell my son he doesn't have a father, because I have experienced how much it hurts to be denied. And love is more important than anything else. I love my wife, I love my son, and I love my father. Goodnight, Papa."

Jess turned to go. When he reached the door, he heard the soft voice behind him:

"Yussel."

He looked back. His father was staring hard at the photograph.

"He has your chin, Yussel," his father said in a quaking voice. He looked up and adjusted his glasses with a trembling hand. "Let us hope he has your eyes too, and not my old weak ones. And yes, let him have your love, as you have mine, my son." He raised the photograph to his lips and kissed it lightly.

And that was all the time it took for Jess to race back to his father and fall into his arms, to be pressed to his chest as if he were a little boy.

The big studio auditorium was packed. This time, though, the audience was not there only for Zany Gray. Jess Robin was no longer unknown. His big first album was behind him. But then he had disappeared for most of a year. There was a mystery about him, and a lively anticipation of his public reappearance.

And so the audience buzzed about his upcoming segment and which of his songs he would sing.

Molly knew. She sat in the front row, their son on her lap. Next to her sat Grandfather Kalmen Rabinovitch, erect on the edge of his seat.

Bubba and the brothers knew, and when the curtain went up, they were on the stage to back up Jess along with the orchestra.

As Jess came onto the stage carrying his guitar, he was greeted by a warm ovation. His eyes roamed over the crowd, sensing its eagerness, which pleased him, and its variety, which pleased him even more deeply, given the song he would sing and its meaning for him.

Then, for a long moment, he fixed his gaze on first Molly and their son, then his father. He smiled at them intimately and with deep pride.

And during those moments before he began, there flashed through his mind all the experiences, all the people, all the lessons that had gone into his composing of his new song, "America."

Then the music welled up behind him, a cathedral of sound, drawing the auditorium tightly to him, and he began:

"Far, we've been travelin' far . . . without a home, but not without a star . . . Free, only want to be free . . . We huddle close, hang onto a dream . . ."

How far they had traveled—his father and those before him, and Jess himself—clinging to their dream.

". . . Home, don't it seem so far away . . . Oh we're travelin' light today . . . in the eye of the storm, in the eye of the storm . . ."

There had been times when he thought he would never find his way back, and when the storm of despair swirled around him, as it must have for so many others searching for the path.

". . . Home, to a new and shiny place . . . Make our bed and we'll say our grace . . . Freedom's light burning warm, freedom's light burning warm . . ."

There was love in the light, and peace, and trust, and Jess sent out the warmth with his voice, and felt it returned to him a thousandfold.

"Everywhere around the world, they're coming to America; every time that flag's unfurled, they're coming to America . . . Got a dream to take them there . . . They're coming to America . . . Got a dream they come to share . . . They're coming to America."

All those ages, all that past, all those generations of cantors and carpenters and cooks and ranchers and musicians and mechanics, they came, and Jess had shared the hope with them, and seen what they had made.

"They're coming to America ... They're coming to America ... They're coming to America ... They're coming to America ... Today ... Today ... Today ... Today ... Today."

Immediately in front of him were the representatives of the generations, the steadfast holders of the dream and the guarantors of its continuity—his father, Molly, his son—with him now.

And as he hit the final chord, "Today!" his right arm shot into the air in a fist of unity, and he lowered his head as if in prayer while the audience rose in exultant praise of his performance, his song, his message. When he opened his eyes, he saw his father now standing at the very edge of the stage, tall and proud, his hands high over his head in applause, tears of love rolling down beneath his glasses.

Jess was, in the most reverent, transcendent sense of the phrase, at last, home free.

ABOUT THE AUTHOR

RICHARD WOODLEY wrote the novel based on the screenplay for *The Bad News Bears* and its two sequels, as well as *Slapshot,* and *The Champ.* A former editor of *Life* magazine, he has had articles published in such magazines as *Esquire, Playboy, Rolling Stone,* and *Atlantic Monthly,* and has published two books of nonfiction. A resident of Manhattan, Richard Woodley is currently at work on a new novel.